JACOB BURAK

DO CHIMPANZEES DREAM OF RETIREMENT

AN ENCOUNTER BETWEEN PSYCOLOGY, EVOLUTION AND BUSINESS

TRANSLATED FROM HEBREW BY EVAN FALLENBERG AND SHIRA ATIK

ISBN: 1452864438
ISBN-13: 9781452864433
Library of Congress Control Number: 2010906966

TABLE OF CONTENTS

PART I:
REAP OR WEEP

Introduction

In 1992, Dr. Reuben Hecht, the chief executive of "Dagon Granaries of Israel," agreed to meet with me. I had been urging him to invest in the venture capital fund I had founded, but he was yet to be convinced. Watching his reaction, I was painfully aware that my arguments were not tugging at his heartstrings, let alone his purse strings. I rattled off a list of respectable investors who were interested in the Evergreen Fund, but nothing moved him. Dr. Hecht – an entrepreneur from a family of entrepreneurs; a private collector of art and archeology; one of the founders of the Haifa University, and a renowned philanthropist – had been able to fulfill his dreams without the help of an investment in venture capital. I was running out of ideas. What could I say that would persuade "Dagon Granaries" to invest in my fund?

And then – perhaps out of politeness – Dr. Hecht changed the subject. He wanted to know about my parents, where they were from, what their story was. Although I failed to see the connection between my family history and venture capital, I was relieved to deviate from our marketing negotiations, which seemed to be shattering into shards – and not the kind that Dr. Hecht collected. I told him that my parents came from eastern Poland, had survived the war and married in Germany. In 1947 they had sailed to Palestine, where their ship was intercepted by the British blockade. They were sent to Cyprus, where I was born in 1948.

Dr. Hecht was ready with the next question. In fact, from the moment I had mentioned my parents' voyage to Palestine, he had been struggling to contain his excitement. "And what was the name of the ship your parents sailed to Israel?" he asked with the German-Jewish restraint that infused his personality. "Do you remember?" To my surprise, I did; usually my memory fails me when I'm under stress. "The *Ben Hecht*," I responded. My host's face lit up. For the first time, I could see a glimmer of understanding in his eyes. The tension that had stretched across his face, from the tip of his small white beard to the top of his broad forehead, was replaced by the calm demeanor of someone who had received all the information he needed. He leaned over to his assistant, who had been there throughout the entire meeting, and whispered in German, "One million." The meeting was over. Dagon Granaries became one of Evergreen's most faithful investors.

I was in shock. It was only later, after a phone call to my mother, that I understood what had just transpired. After World War II, she told me, right before the birth of the Jewish state, there were a number of different – and conflicting – political groups. These groups funded the ships that were used to rescue those Jews who were still in Europe. The connection between the ship's passengers and the ideological affiliations of their sponsors was powerful. Ben Hecht (no relation to Dr. Hecht) was an author, a prolific screenwriter (he had won two Oscars), and a committed right-wing Zionist activist. The ship that bore his

name was one of the last of its kind to make its way to
Israel in 1947.

Dr. Hecht's political leanings were familiar to anyone
who had spent even a moment in his company. He was a
fervent Revisionist, and had served as the personal advisor to right-wing Prime Ministers Menachem Begin and
Yitzchak Shamir. My parents, on the other hand, had only
ended up on the *Ben Hecht* due to an extraordinary series
of coincidences. They did not share the right-wing views
of their shipmates.

A year after our meeting, Dr. Hecht passed away. I
played the scene of our meeting over and over in my mind.
The more I thought about it, the more I became convinced
of the phenomenon that I had encountered many times
before and would encounter many times since: that business decisions, particularly those regarding investments,
are susceptible to all kinds of emotional influences, some
of which prevail over reason.

Dr. Hecht, full of good will but clueless about venture capital investments, was desperately searching for a
hook on which to hang his decision. He was looking for
a sense of connection, of tribalism, of belonging. His behavior may not have been rational, but it was supremely
human.

I have had hundreds of business meetings since then,
and in every case, I knew what I was selling. Only rarely,
however, did I know what the person sitting across from
me was buying. I was selling a good return on their
investments, but the investors (especially those who
were Jewish) were buying a variety of commodities: a
feeling of involvement, of taking a part in Israel's high-
tech drama, a business venture that would offset their

charitable donations to Israel, even a desire to ensure future employment for their children. And therein lies the magic: business isn't numbers, business is people.

૭෴ා

I can't say that my life-long dream was to become a businessman. When I finished high school, I was drafted into an academic unit of the army, to my parents' unconcealed delight. In the application form, I checked off psychology as my preferred field of study, followed by industrial engineering. My father took one look at the form, then stared at me intently. There was no need for words; after all those years of silence, he was quite proficient at non-verbal expression. His message was clear: "My son will study something practical, and he will find a profession that is risk-free and secure."

I didn't deliberate for long; as the only son of Holocaust survivors, I was eager to please my parents. In 1970, I graduated from the Faculty of Industrial and Management Engineering at the Technion – Israel's highest Institute of Technology. Psychology was put on the back burner. I spent the next three years as the head of a small planning unit in the navy, and then got involved in some fascinating projects of operations research for the navy's chief commander.

Despite feeling extremely comfortable with statistics and quantitative models, I was never really drawn to the world of business. In truth, I didn't believe that I could succeed as a businessman. The consulting firm that I co-founded with a partner was the most extensive business venture I could think of. Analysis? Yes. Consulting?

Absolutely. But the thought of risking my own funds, much less those of other people, seemed unfeasible.

In the fall of 1984, I underwent a unique experience that changed my entire approach to business. Not long before, two companies had bought out 40% of my consulting firm. As part of the deal, I asked them to send me to the executive program at the Harvard Business School, since I had never studied business management. My request was approved, and the course turned out to be the most enriching experience of my professional life.

Classes at Harvard are structured around the presentation and analysis of actual case studies of different corporations. Students review a case study before class, and the professor acts as the moderator of the ensuing discussion. Only rarely does the class reach an unequivocal consensus. The exchange of ideas is as important as any one point of view, and the opinions of the students, all of whom come from general management backgrounds, are as valuable as the opinions of the professor. Your class standing is largely determined by your equally ambitious classmates.

During the fourteen-week course we reviewed no fewer than two hundred case studies, beginning with quality control issues in a small South American water-pump factory, and ending with the marketing strategy of General Electric. One case study presented the history of Allied Chemicals, which I consider to be the story of its manager, John Connor. In 1962, Allied, which specialized in chemical manufacturing, began to acquire gas and oil properties in Texas, mostly to provide raw materials to its operation. In the early 1970s, this investment strategy was largely supported by the company's newly appointed general manager, Connor. The story of the new manager's relationship with his long-time conservative board members was presented in the case study at length and in great detail. It seemed that his decision to drop some of Allied's traditional but less profitable activities did not go over well with his board of directors. In a series of events that attest to Connor's business vision, and to what seemed to me, his frustration with his board, Allied invested significant funds in gas and oil explorations throughout the continent, at the expense of its more established but ailing businesses.

The case study ended here. The students were not told how the investments worked out, how Allied evolved, and what happened to Connor. Professor Michael Y. Yoshino, who facilitated this discussion, asked the class to rate the manager's decisions on a scale of 1 to 5. The average score was less than three; I gave him a four. I sympathized with the painful loneliness of a talented manager who, I felt, was being prevented by his fossilized board members from leading his company to new horizons.

Professor Yoshino then provided us with one additional piece of information: a large portion of the investment funds were earmarked for a minority position in an oil exploration project in the North Sea, a region that was far away from most of the company's activities. If all went well, Allied stood to benefit a great deal, but there was no way it could supervise the project; this would be the role of the majority owner. After sharing this additional fact with us, the professor asked for another vote. This time, the average score declined to two. I gave him a five – the only one of the 80 students to do so. Professor Yoshino looked at me enigmatically, and then went on to tell us how the case resolved itself. In 1979, when Edward Hennessey took over the management of Allied, the gas and oil businesses that Connor had developed were responsible for 80% of the company's sales, and for much of its profit. (Connor, by the way, went on to become the Secretary of Trade under Lyndon Johnson, and was the first senior member of the administration to resign as a result of his objection to the Vietnam War. Again, he had shown himself to be an independent thinker and a person of integrity.)

I have contemplated this story many times since then, and I can honestly say that it influenced my decision to go into business. Even if I couldn't fully appreciate Connor's business acumen, I identified with the loneliness he must have felt vis-à-vis what seemed to be an antagonistic board of directors, and I respected the courage it took for him to implement a strategy that he alone believed in. He did his best to lead a company that boasted tremendous financial resources but had limited management potential, and ultimately his decisions proved themselves to be correct.

Empathy – the ability to put oneself in someone else's shoes and to feel what he feels – may be the single most important asset in business. As long as you know what it is you're selling, empathy will allow you to know what the other person is buying.

Like other essential business traits, empathy is rooted in human weakness – in this case, sensitivity and vulnerability. Because we need to evaluate the other person's motives (to make sure he isn't hostile), we develop the ability to put ourselves in that person's shoes. I wouldn't have been able to go into business, nor would I advise anyone else to do so, before mastering this ability.

What is Success, Anyway?

I suspect that this book would never have been written, much less read, had I not succeeded in business. Personally, this, like being included in one or another list of the most wealthy, gives me no gratification. As far as I'm concerned, success means only one thing: the freedom to live my life in my own way.

The secret of success, in my opinion, is that there is no secret, and whoever gets to the "top" knows that there is no top. The hardest decision for a successful businessman to make is to relinquish the colossal skill of making money to make room for a more balanced life, one of humility and commitment to non-business related causes.

The only secret I know is the one revealed by American playwright Tennessee Williams. "Success is shy," he wrote. "It won't come out when you're watching." And in spite of this sound advice, thousands of entrepreneurs, advisors and business writers promise to let their readers in on the secret of success, the one that was revealed to them when they dared to look for it. The question never asked when discussing "the secret of success" is this: how do you define success, anyway?

The reason for this omission is simple. In the Western culture of materialism, the definition of success is clear: ownership of assets, ideally liquid assets. How this wealth is attained is beside the point. The cost of success is equally irrelevant: the thousands of hours and days spent away from family and friends, an unhealthy lifestyle that deprives a person of the rest and nutrition he needs, and worst of all, the need to compromise on one's values. Those who climb the ladder of success often neglect to check the value-related stability of the building against which the ladder is leaning.

One of my investors once told me that surgeons could be divided into two groups. The first group consists of natural surgeons. These are the doctors who are as energized at the end of a procedure as they were at the beginning, the ones who hurry home because they don't want to miss out on the evening's activities. The surgeons in the second group are exhausted at the end of an operation, and rush home so that they can collapse into oblivion. These are the non-natural surgeons. The most interesting aspect of this comparison is that there is no difference in the quality of their work.

I believe that businessmen too can be divided into two categories: natural businessmen, who are so caught up in their work that they are always surprised when it's time to go home; and non-natural businessmen, for whom the end of the day never comes soon enough. Despite their vastly different personalities, the two groups can be equally successful. Natural businessmen are extroverted, sociable, and energetic; the non-natural ones compensate for the lack of these qualities with self-discipline, patience, perseverance and acuity. I know that I belong to the second group. If I were to hang a plaque over my desk, it would be inscribed with a quote from Olympic medalist James Kunkel, a rower who won gold medals in both Sydney and Athens: "If I had eight hours to chop down trees, I would spend six of them sharpening the axe."

Most business people, in my opinion, are non-natural and wouldn't have set foot in the financial world at all if business didn't play such a leading role in our culture. For people like them, the key to success is, to a large extent, a matter of choosing the right industry. Businesses that depend on honed managerial skills, politicians, and regulators do not suit them, nor do businesses with low barriers to entry. This is the stomping ground of the "naturals."

On the other hand, a company that focuses on the financial needs of investors is an excellent choice for non-natural businessmen. Fees in the venture capital industry are globally determined (2%-3% of committed capital and 20% of the profit) and could survive even the infamous bargaining tactics of the most strident financial institutions. By picking the right technology, start-ups can yield tens of millions of dollars to fund managers. And, above all, the client is generally an astute professional who understands the rules of the game, and whose loyalty to a good investment manager is strong.

By founding Evergreen, I chose to focus on private equity investments. It is a combination of two main activities: fundraising and investment. The qualities needed to succeed in these two areas are fundamentally different, although patience is crucial for both.

In 1987, when I went to Canada to raise capital for Evergreen's first fund, I kept a written log of every telephone call and every meeting. During the nine months I spent on and off there, I made over two thousand phone calls and met with about three hundred people, some of them more than once. In the end, I recruited twenty-one investors, who together invested four million Canadian dollars. That was all I had to start with. At times, the recruitment process seemed futile, and at one point, when a major investor, and a friend, decided not to invest in Evergreen, I nearly gave up. Then I remembered the words of Thomas Edison, the inventor of the electric light bulb: "Most great people have attained their greatest success just one step beyond their greatest failure." Intelligence, perseverance and patience, I learned, were even more important than talent.

The last twenty-four hours of the fundraising process reminded me of the rigorous trials designed by the powerful Greek gods to purify the souls of mortals. The motifs of these mythological plays – loyalty and treachery, greediness and generosity – are the same emotions that showed up in the modern-day drama of my fundraising.

After many years of experience, I am convinced that some of the more savvy investors reasoned that if I had put as much diligence and thoughtfulness into investments as I was putting into fundraising, their money might not disappear, at least not right away. The hope was that I would be able to postpone the inevitable crash long enough to shield them from embarrassment when they bumped into their more skeptical colleagues who had decided not to invest.

But even those fund managers who choose the right industry cannot succeed without luck. Where would I be today if I hadn't become involved, early on in my career, in a particularly lucrative investment? The million and a half dollars that Evergreen invested in Geotek, an up-and-coming wireless communications company, earned us $22 million – almost the entire net worth of Evergreen at the time. Many of the people who were inspired by Evergreen to invest in Geotek did very well, and as a result became loyal investors in Evergreen. Don't believe anyone who prides himself on his ability to buy or sell just when the global economy is on the verge of change – not unless his middle name is Luck. How else could I explain the excellence of Evergreen's investment managers? Or my partnership with Ofer Neeman, whom I met by chance? Twenty-four-carat pure luck.

Most of the people who zealously read through the media's lists of the wealthiest people do not realize that these lists are biased toward the survivors. The people who make the lists are the ones who managed to survive in a world where success is like a balloon surrounded by children wielding pins. Thousands of bankrupt individuals and business failures have fallen by the wayside. For some strange reason, however, we tend to blame our failures on bad luck, while taking all the credit for our successes.

In business, luck is when something very unlikely actually occurs. Perhaps we won an unexpected bid, or sat next to a potential investor on the airplane. Maybe a change in the currency rate benefited our leading export market. It could be a natural disaster that indirectly results in a meteoric rise in the sales of our product, or a change in the land designation of a site we had bought twenty years earlier. Sometimes it's a combination of events. A modest degree of success can be attributed to talent and hard work, but the legendary successes are always a result of statistical variance that acts as a tailwind in the market. Or in other words, luck.

The naturals in business will find their way to success regardless of the circumstances, but for the rest of us, the path to fortune tends to be a long and exhausting one, and luck can make the journey much less arduous. In many cases, we would never have reached our destination without it.

The colorful British media tycoon Felix Dennis is a natural businessman. As far as he's concerned, the surface of the earth is covered with billions of pound notes, some of which have his name on them. All he has to do is collect them. In fact, according to the London Times 2006 list of the richest people, he has gathered about six hundred million of them. In his crudely titled book "How to Get Rich," he compares the process of moneymaking to drug addiction. Nobody ever thought that exercise could become addictive, he explains, until science discovered the endorphins that we release when we exercise. "And believe me," he concludes, "making money is much more addictive than jogging."

But wait. If making money can be as addictive as drugs, perhaps we can define success in terms of sacrifice. Are we willing to sacrifice clear-mindedness, balance, and objectivity? What about spending time with the people whose company we most enjoy? Or investing in self-enrichment? Whether we are addicted to money or to drugs, the results are the same: we are willing to sacrifice a lot to give us our fix. Maybe we should really define success as the ability to wean ourselves from our addiction to making money, and from the "high" that we get when we succeed.

For the natural businessperson and entrepreneur, one of the keys to success is a feeling of ownership. Dennis, for instance, would rather lose one of his fingers than give up a small percentage of his shares in any of his major companies. My own experience is exactly the opposite. Every time I gave up a portion of my assets, the remainder grew at an astonishing rate. When you share your success with the tax authorities in a way that ensures your peace of mind, you'd be surprised at the rate the rest of your money will increase. Many years ago, I made a rule for myself:

I would never accept or reject a business deal simply for tax purposes. For me, the amount of money I could save as a result of complicated tax planning is not worth the emotional energy and the moral uneasiness that go along with it.

Right before Evergreen went private in 1998, I decided to divide the shares equally between myself and the CEO, Ofer Neeman. This unconventional decision forged a strong bond between the two of us that led the company to a level of success that would not have been possible otherwise. For non-natural businessmen, finding the right partner is one of the keys to success. The relationship between Ofer and me allowed both of us to utilize our individual strengths and to make balanced decisions. To this day, more than ten years after our partnership began, we do not have a written contract; our business is built solely on trust. A good partnership enriches a business relationship, just as a bad one sours it. If, like me, you're not a natural businessman, then find a good partner. The bottom line is that what matters isn't how many shares you'll be giving away, but the kind of person you're giving them to.

∽

Plenty of people dream of success, but only a few manage to stay awake long enough to do the hard work that is required. The scale of a person's fantasies is inversely proportional to his success. One of the more common fantasies is called, "If only I could meet so-and-so." You fill in the blank: Donald Trump, Bill Gates, Steven Spielberg…. These dreamers are convinced that if they could only meet their hero, they could win him over with their personal charm, and impress him with their business vision. The end result, of course, is that their hero would lead them on to wealth and success.

I've met many of these "dream team" heroes over the years. (In one of my drawers, I have a photograph of me standing between Bill Gates and Sheldon Adelson.)

A warning to dreamers: if you ever do get to meet your hero, be aware that his instinct is to find the flaws in every proposal he hears. Simply put, the busier a person is, the more he will look for a reason to decline a proposal rather than a reason to accept it. Furthermore, after a person has attained a certain degree of success, he usually wants to narrow the scope of his personal investments rather than expand it. And he is, quite openly, prepared to forego a business opportunity in order to avoid complicating his already complicated life. For most of these people, the chance of doubling or tripling a one-million-dollar investment in your venture is just not worth the effort, never mind the risk.

༄

The story of the business world is the story of the people who make it work. This long compendium of stories includes many accounts of human weakness. If everyone behaved entirely rationally, the stock market would grind to a complete halt. Nobody would buy or sell even a single share. For every intelligent (but human) seller who believes that the stock is selling high, there is an equally intelligent (but human) buyer who believes that the stock is a steal.

Thousands of studies in human behavioral science explain how our inherent biases determine the borders of the business playgrounds we all play in. How else can you explain the following phenomena?

> We are more likely to respond to e-mails when the sender's initials are the same as ours. We buy more stock on sunny days. We focus on the short-term, despite understanding that it is in our best interest to focus on the long-term. We are seduced by stories rather than facts. We see economic trends where they don't actually exist. We are evolutionarily blind to small probabilities but nonetheless exercise optimism and over-confidence in our daily conduct, even when the odds are strongly against us. For the very same evolutionary reasons, we are fearful for our status, and are therefore willing to take unreasonable risks to stave off our status anxiety. We work night and day to achieve freedom of choice, but suffer when there are too many options to choose from. We are willing to sacrifice a great deal in order to be rich, but we cannot internalize the fact that money cannot buy happiness, and that focusing on material values is actually an obstacle to happiness. We kill ourselves so that we can retire in comfort, without realizing that it is easier to get rich than it is to retire.

Two thirds of what we do is based on what everyone else does, half of our choices are dictated by our genetic makeup. Our birth order and the environment in which we are raised take another chunk out of our free will.

At the very least, let us attempt to distinguish between what we can actually choose for ourselves, and what only appears to be a matter of free choice.

TO HAVE OR TO BE: THAT IS THE QUESTION

∾

"The dictionary is the only place where success comes before work."

-Vince Lombardi, football coach

Rich and Happy – Only in Fairytales

In June 2004, James Montier, who was at the time the senior global equity strategist of the German investment bank Dresdner Kleinworth, surprised his clients and colleagues. Montier, who had gained a reputation for himself as a bearish investor, admitted that even he became depressed when reading his own research reports. As a result, he decided to focus that month's report on another issue entirely: happiness, with a capital H. Montier clearly enjoyed a high status within the bank: "Money does not buy happiness," he dared to write, and instead of giving his readers the financial tips they were waiting for, he challenged them to take inventory of their inner lives. Anyone who was hoping for an update on the hottest stocks of the summer had to struggle with the unequivocal discovery that monetary success did not lead to happiness. Readers looking for monetary guidance learned instead that the more one cares about money, the less happy that person will be. The pursuit of happiness is a concept as old as man. In spite of its central role in human culture, psychology has always preferred to study the negative aspects of our emotions. Joy? Satisfaction? Happiness? Forget them. Researchers have shown that since 1887, only one out of every 14 psychological articles deals with the brighter side of life. The rest focus on anger, fear, and depression.

Lately, however, the tide has begun to turn. Behavioral science now includes a relatively new area, happiness research, which has already attracted some of the most prominent researchers. Daniel Kahneman, who won the Nobel Prize in Economics in 2002, Ed Diener of the University of Illinois, and Daniel Gilbert of Harvard University are some of the leading researchers who, in a relatively short amount of time, have developed some important concepts to help us in our search for happiness.

All of this breakthrough research became possible once it was established that happiness could be measured. The part of our brain that controls happiness is located on the left side of the brain, near the forehead. People who sustain a head injury in this area tend to be more depressed. Conversely, people with a high level of electric activity in this part of the brain, even when they're at rest, are generally happier.

Much to everyone's relief, researchers are able to conduct valid studies of happiness without attaching electrodes to anybody's head. The questionnaires used by the majority of the researchers have proven to be quite reliable. Some of the questionnaires ask respondents to rank themselves on a scale of one to seven on a number of questions, such as "How would you rate your happiness in comparison to that of others?" Other surveys ask respondents to rate how strongly they identify with a series of sentences, such as "If I could live my life again, I wouldn't change a thing," or "I have fulfilled most of my goals." Mood samples, in which the patient is electronically prompted to describe his mood every few hours, are another tool used to measure happiness.

Would you like to find out how happy you are? Nothing could be simpler. Martin Seligman, the guru of positive psychology and happiness research, set up a website with more than a dozen self-evaluation quizzes, many of which are quite straightforward. If you go to www. authentichappiness.com and fill out any of the questionnaires, you will immediately learn how your happiness level compares with that of the thousands of people who took the quiz before you.

The conclusions of these studies are not at all surprising. Those who tested as "happy" were more satisfied in every realm. Socially, they were more likely to get married and less likely to divorce, and they tended to have a wider, more supportive network of friends. Professionally, happiness was associated with creativity, effectiveness, decision-making ability, job quality, and ultimately a higher income. Personally, happy people live longer and have stronger immune systems.

A study that analyzed the 1932 diaries of nuns in the Notre Dame Seminary in America found that those sisters who wrote frequently about their happy experiences went on to live significantly longer than their less prolific classmates. Oscar Award winners live an average of 4 ½ years longer than nominees who didn't go on to win. Nobel Prize winners between 1900 and 1950 lived two years more than their colleagues who were candidates but didn't win.

What can we do, then, to maximize our happiness and reap all its rewards? Although this seems to be a straightforward question, in order to understand the answer we have to be familiar with the basic components of happiness. Once we understand what constitutes happiness, we will have a better chance of controlling each individual factor.

The first ingredient of happiness – and the most influential – is immutable: our genes. Each of us was born with a genetic happiness setpoint. This was confirmed in a study by University of Minnesota Professor David Lykken. Lykken collected data on hundreds of pairs of identical twins who were born in Minnesota between 1936 and 1955. He measured their levels of happiness, and found that the results for one twin could predict, with uncanny accuracy, the results for the other twin. After comparing this data with a parallel study of fraternal twins, he determined that a person's genetic makeup is responsible for 50% of his or her happiness. According to the study, the similarity between identical twins who were separated at birth and grew up in different environments was the same as the similarity between identical twins who grew up in the same house. Fifty percent is the magic number for the influence of genes on a whole litany of conditions: schizophrenia, manic-depression, alcoholism, and criminal malfeasance.

It is extremely difficult to offset our genetic predispositions. Although a lucky streak, or an unfortunate accident, can influence our happiness, the effect is only temporary. Within a short time, we return to our predetermined level of happiness. A well-known experiment from 1978 examined a group of lottery winners. After a year, they were not much happier than the members of the control group, who had never won the lottery. Similarly, victims of car accidents didn't need more than a year to return to their normative level of happiness. In other words, anyone who is looking for genetic assistance to improve his odds of happiness should find other parents.

The second ingredient that determines our happiness is our circumstances. Age, gender, geography, demographics – these are all circumstantial factors. The role of age, for instance, is familiar to anyone who works in venture capital; it is referred to as the J curve. Young people, by and large, are relatively happy. As they age, their level of happiness steadily declines, reaching its low point in a person's thirties, then gradually increasing once again. After age sixty, the level of happiness reaches its peak. Evidently, older people have attained their goals or have come to terms with their limitations and adjusted their expectations accordingly.

Apparently, intelligence and education have no real influence on an individual's happiness. As French author Gustav Flaubert quipped, "Stupidity, selfishness and good health are the three requirements of happiness, though if stupidity is lacking, all is lost."

Other more fluid circumstances include family, career, job security, faith, income, and health. Numerous studies have shown that people who are married, healthy, economically secure, and – especially – members of a faith-based community, report higher levels of happiness. The most influential factor in a person's happiness is one's familial and social situation. A decrease in salary, as long as it doesn't prevent us from meeting our basic needs, plays a very minor role in our happiness.

The most important discovery, however, about the affect of circumstantial factors on our happiness, isn't about one factor or another, but about the aggregated extent to which they influence our internal happiness.

It turns out that no more than 10% of our emotional well-being is determined by circumstance.

At first glance, this fact is surprising. In a capitalistic society, where material status is so important, we would have expected a much higher correlation. However, there are numerous forces that counterbalance the influence of circumstantial factors. One of these is the phenomenon known as hedonistic adaptation – our staggering ability to acclimate. No matter what hand life deals us, we adapt to it with remarkable ease. With the exception of losing a loved one or being unemployed, both of which can affect our wellbeing for a longer period, changes become normative relatively quickly. Any new development in our lives will influence our degree of satisfaction at first, but within a short time we adapt to it. Contentedness or disappointment, success or failure – these are determined by our most recent experience. In the language of physics, satisfaction has a short half-life.

Hedonistic adaptation is a very comforting coping mechanism, a kind of psychological vaccine. Its origins are evolutionary and its job is to safeguard our emotional wellbeing during trying times, to shield us from anguish and unhappiness. The ability to adapt to difficult situations ensures that we will not stray too far from our genetic setpoint. But there is a flip side, too. The same mechanism that saves us from despair also guards us from excessive happiness. The moment we experience an elevation in our mood, hedonistic adaptation steps in and brings us down to our normal level of happiness.

And money? Of all the variables, we tend to assume that there is a strong correlation between wealth and happiness. However, even wealth cannot stand up to hedonistic adaptation. The happiness that comes with getting a raise, for example, is very short-lived. Our new salary quickly becomes the norm, the new standard for future reference. Nowhere is this clearer than in the relative happiness of residents of the United States, the country that has elevated consumerism to nearly religious heights. Even though the buying power of Americans has more than doubled in the last three decades, the level of satisfaction among Americans is disappointingly static. Sadly, the crime rate, the divorce rate, and the level of alcoholism have all risen in direct proportion to the average income.

I first met Professor Daniel Gilbert at a 2003 conference at MIT. Sitting on stage were a group of some of the top scientific minds in the country, and an order of Buddhist monks led by the Dalai Lama, whose teachings are described in his book, *The Art of Happiness*. Gilbert, a professor of psychology, is best known as the author of *Stumbling on Happiness*, a 2006 bestseller. He agreed to share some of his wisdom with me in a telephone conversation that took place about a year after the conference.

"Money is important," said Professor Gilbert, "but only insofar as it enables us to meet our basic needs. In terms of its impact on happiness, the difference between no income and an annual income of $40,000 is huge. The difference between $10 million and $50 million dollars, however, is negligible, if it exists at all." Part of Gilbert's scientific research revolves around this concept.

Human beings, argues Gilbert, are the only creatures who can mentally travel through time and imagine how they would feel in different scenarios. Most of our expectations for happiness are based on images that we create in our heads: the long-awaited moment when we first step into our brand-new car, or frolic on the golden sands of the Caribbean Islands, or shake hands with our boss when he offers us a raise. In these forecasts, accuracy is essential; without it, the gap between our predictions and reality can have a profound effect on our happiness.

However, a groundbreaking study by Professor Gilbert and Professor Tim Wilson of the University of Virginia shows that our forecasts of the future are far from accurate. According to the study, we are particularly bad at predicting our future emotions: good things are never as good as we imagine they'll be, and bad things are never as bad. We think of ourselves as much more vulnerable than we really are, while also believing that it doesn't take much to make us happy. We think that a new job or a new relationship will change our lives forever. In truth, however, they raise our spirits for a relatively short time. Similarly, we are much hardier than we think. Our ability to overcome traumatic situations is almost always better than we had predicted.

This phenomenon, which researchers call the Impact Bias, explains why it is so hard for us to be happy. Our excessively high expectations make it hard for us to enjoy the good things that happen in our lives. Nonetheless, Gilbert admits that this disparity also serves a positive purpose. If entrepreneurs could accurately predict their future earnings, and were less optimistic, they would never risk founding a new business.

So how can money overcome human nature? It can't. Money can't buy happiness, says Professor Gilbert, but the judicious use of money can help. "If happiness is really their goal," he says, "then most people are not using their money properly."

And what is the right way to handle money? Gilbert, who directs the Harvard Center for Happiness, suggests three general rules:

1. Use your money in small installments, for things that will enhance your daily life. Avoid any major expenditure, which will give you satisfaction that is intense but short-lived, as it is exposed to hedonistic adaptation.

2. Invest your money in experiences rather than in material possessions. Buy tickets to a performance rather than clothing; spend your money on a vacation rather than on a fancy watch. Experiences, as opposed to objects, are less vulnerable to hedonistic adaptation. Experiences have another advantage over acquisitions, in that we are often able to embellish the experience when we remember it. To a large extent, our identity is made up of our experiences.

3. Use your money to work less, not to buy more. Make time for social relationships. The correlation between a strong network of friends and happiness is extremely high.

There is an old adage that teaches us that "consumerism leads to happiness – anybody who cannot attain happiness hasn't consumed enough." According to Gilbert, the central mythology of Western culture – that money leads to happiness – is, at best, unfounded, and at worst, an example of cultural and economic fraud on a very large scale. His message to advertisers and marketers is clear:

the next time you want to promote a new product, promise anything you want, except happiness.

To the dismay of Gilbert and his colleagues, more and more young people continue to believe that money is the most important goal in life (see chart).

Changing priorities: money counts

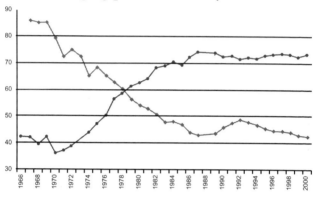

Percentage of college freshmen who rate these goals as "essential" or "very important."

—♦— develop meaningful philosophy of live   —•— become well off financially

Source: HERI (http://www.gsels.ucla.edu/heri/heri.html)

An ongoing study led by the University of California examines the changing values of students who had just been admitted. This study, which has been around since the late 1960s, has involved over 200,000 students to date. In the early 1970s, 80% of the students ranked "developing a meaningful philosophy of life" as their most important value. Only 40% believed that wealth was a priority. Today, however, these numbers are reversed.

This begs the question: is there a correlation between our values and our ability to be happy? In 2000, Ed Diener and S. Ushi studied 7,167 undergraduates from 41 states.

The researchers wanted to find out whether a person's existential priorities could influence their level of happiness. The results of the study (which was called "Love or Money?") offer some solace to those who are troubled by our culture's preoccupation with wealth. Those who ranked money as one of their top priorities reported a lower level of happiness, whereas those who were more concerned with love reported a greater degree of satisfaction.

Love or Money?

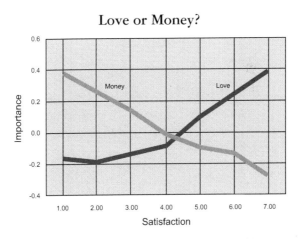

Source: Diener & Oishi, 2000

Additional studies confirm that those who are driven by a desire for fame and fortune are less content than those who are driven by a desire for good relationships and personal growth, even when their material desires are fulfilled. And if that's not convincing enough, researchers Cohen and Cohen discovered, in a 1995 study, that the people who cared most about material things were more likely than others to suffer from an assortment of mental disturbances: paranoia (43% more), narcissism (40% more), substance abuse (34% more), and communication disorders (53% more).

Some of the surprising findings about individual happiness have already overflowed into the realm of economic research, which focuses on collective wellbeing. On a national level, the connection between wealth and happiness is undeniable: it is fair to say that citizens of wealthy countries tend to be happier than citizens of poor countries (see chart). However, we have to take other variables into account. First of all, richer countries are more likely to be democracies with well-developed individual rights, health care, and other services. These institutions contribute to national happiness, which diminishes the relative importance of monetary wealth.

Subjective well-being by level of economic development

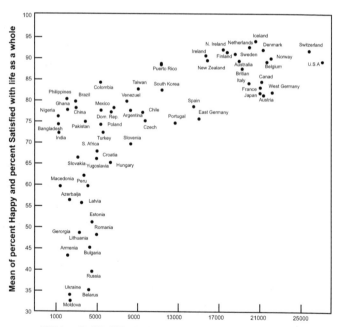

GNP / capita (World Bank purchasing power partly estimates, 1995 U.S.

Source: R. Inglehartand H.D. Klingemann "Genes, Culture and Happiness," MIT Press, 2000.

Even a quick scan of the chart shows that once the average income exceeds $25,000 a year, more money does not bring more happiness. On a national level, "the happiness paradox," as defined by Richard Layard, lies in the fact that societies that seek and provide greater income are little if any happier than before. At the same time, in the Third World, where extra income really brings increased happiness, income levels are very low while in the First World, there is more depression, more alcoholism and more crime than fifty years ago.

Politicians, for their part, hijacked the concept of GNP that since its inception in the 1930s has served as an economic tool to measure unemployment and economic cycles. The idea that GNP would represent national happiness proved false.

In fact, data collected by a subcommittee of the British Parliament revealed that even though the GNP in the United Kingdom had risen sharply in the last several decades, the happiness of their citizens has not improved. Strangely enough, the citizens of poorer countries such as Mexico, Nigeria, Venezuela and Colombia are happy in spite of their national GNP.

Readers of the Wall Street Journal may not find this surprising. In August of 2004, the newspaper reported a similar discovery. Participants in a research study were asked to rank their happiness on a scale of 1 to 7. Based on this information, researchers learned that the residents of Calcutta were at the 4.6 level on the happiness scale, only 1.2 points behind the richest people of the Fortune 400 list.

One person who will surely not be surprised is the king of Bhutan, the tiny kingdom perched atop the Himalaya Mountains, whose subjects have long been among the happiest in the world. Many years ago, King Gigama Singeya Wangchuk did away with the GNP altogether, replacing it with a National Happiness Measure. He also banned television in his kingdom. (When this ban was lifted in 1999, Bhutan immediately experienced a rise in crime and addiction.) Western scientists are beginning to follow in his footsteps. Professor Daniel Kahneman and other researchers are trying to implement a National Happiness Index in the United States to give them a better understanding of the happiness of American citizens, and how successful their government is in promoting happiness.

So why doesn't the level of national happiness increase with income? Why is it that when individuals become richer than their peers, they are happier, but when an entire community attains greater wealth, their level of happiness doesn't increase at all, at least not in the Western world? Psychologist Abraham Maslow helped answer this question with the Maslow Hierarchy of Needs. This concept lists five levels, ranging from the need for food and sex, through the need for physical security, to the need for self-fulfillment. Residents of Western countries, who take their physical security for granted, are constantly striving to attain the next level up on the hierarchy. Thus, while their needs change, their level of dissatisfaction remains the same.

Behavioral scientists provided the other part of the answer when they overwhelmingly proved that most people view wealth in relative terms, and that the role of comparison here is crucial. Harvard students who participated in a 1998 study developed by Solnick and Hemenway affirmed that they would rather earn $50,000 a year while their friends earned $25,000 a year, than earn $100,000 a year while their friends earned twice as much. It can be said, then, that one person's gain is another person's emotional loss. In reality, we compare ourselves to a narrow group of no more than 150 people – our school friends, people we graduated university with, a small circle of acquaintances, our coworkers, relatives. One hundred and fifty seems to be a magic number: that was the size of our ancestral tribes in the African savanna. One hundred and fifty is also the maximum number of people that we can refer to emotionally and intellectually. The centrality of comparison cannot be denied: one study shows that if a woman's sister's husband earns more than her own husband, she is much more likely to look for a job.

Olympic medalists were not immune to the researcher's curiosity, either. Twenty years after a competition, bronze medalists were happier than silver medalists. Silver medalists compared themselves to the gold medalists that they might have been, while bronze medalists compared themselves to the athletes who didn't come away with any medal at all.

A study that compared the happiness of East Germans and West Germans immediately after their unification revealed that the happiness of the East Germans rose significantly. Several years later, however, their happiness level began to decline, until it was even lower than their happiness level had been before the two countries combined. The explanation for this is simple: When the Berlin Wall first fell, the East Germans were comparing themselves to residents of other Communist countries, and felt superior, but within a short time they began to compare themselves to West Germans, which made them feel inferior. It is not surprising that the poorer countries in the chart on page 36, which scored relatively high on the happiness scale, had less income inequality.

Bertrand Russell, in *The Conquest of Happiness*, explained this phenomenon lucidly: "Beggars aren't jealous of millionaires. They're jealous of other beggars who are slightly better off."

The implications of this data are radical. Economic growth – the catchphrase of most Western politicians – is one of the factors that determine a country's rank in the international pecking order. However, if the connection between GNP and happiness is so flimsy, the scale becomes meaningless. Moreover, most Western countries function on a decidedly capitalistic system, and the race for wealth and status that is endemic to the free market is a zero-sum game. The number of top positions in any given field is limited, and one person's promotion or raise is, by definition, his colleague's loss.

It is important to bear in mind that because wealthy people are at the top of the social ladder, there are more individuals for them to look down upon. Poor people, on the other hand, can only look up. These comparisons are the primary reason that people who have already attained wealth tend to be happier. In contrast, people who are on their way up the social ladder meet many people who are richer than they are, which adversely affects their happiness.

Given all of this, what can the government do to meet the most basic need of its constituents: happiness?

Traditionally, government has had its own convoluted approach. By raising income taxes and inheritance taxes for the wealthy, the government has been able to raise the happiness level of the less wealthy (which constitutes the majority of the electorate). The average citizen, then, will feel much better off in comparison to the society's elite.

The other, more effective way is to focus on the paradox that drives the global market, which is this: owning more objects and assets does not make people happier in the long run. Our culture cannot seem to accept this. On the contrary, we persuade ourselves that these unnecessary goods and services will, in fact, make us happier. To some extent, the entire economy is built around this paradox.

Consumerism as a value permeated Western culture when our reliance on faith and interpersonal trust plummeted. It filled a vacuum. Over the last fifty years, the level of faith in the United States and England has declined by 50%. The notion of communal responsibility has virtually disappeared. The number of Western citizens who believe that God intervenes in their lives has shrunk almost as much. With the loss of faith, and the rejection of divine punishment, the road was cleared for the culture of consumerism. We find ourselves tyrannized – at least psychologically – by a gargantuan network of commercial and social conventions that have nothing whatsoever to do with happiness.

No Western government so far has been able to stand up to the inflated marketing power of the global businesses which promote consumerism. Similarly, nobody has been able to limit advertising space in the printed media, an action which would not only make its readers happier, but would also help conserve the world's resources. Because businesses are so much richer and more powerful than governments, the needs of the corporations trump the happiness of the individual.

Happiness at last

If our genetic make-up is immutable, and external circumstances are susceptible to adaptation, is it at all possible for us to become happier?

Yes, if we use the third ingredient of Montier's happiness pie, which is responsible for 40% of our potential happiness: discovering which activities make us happy. The good news is that these are all in our control.

In order to document this list, I walked – very gingerly – in the footsteps of psychologist David Myers of Hope College. I culled his most salient recommendations, and added a few to those appearing in his book *The Pursuit of Happiness*. This is how the list was developed.

Nothing on this list requires money. Sleep, researchers will tell you, is much more important than money. Moreover, as we have already seen, the belief that money and happiness are intertwined is not only false, but counterproductive.

And so: try to reconstruct your happiest experience of this past week. What was it? A nice meal with friends? Unusually good sex? A show, a movie, a great book? None of these, of course, has anything to do with currency fluctuation or a rise in gas prices.

Here's an abbreviated version of the guide to happiness:

1. Recognize that economic success does not lead to happiness. People adapt to changing circumstances; and wealth, like physical incapacity, belongs in this category. Economic need leads to distress, but wealth does not guarantee happiness.
2. Exercise regularly. Exercise can help cure mild depression; it energizes the body and the mind. During exercise, our body releases endorphins, which are natural pain-fighters that are chemically related to morphine. This is the reason many athletes report an improvement in their mood when they work out for more than twenty minutes.
3. Have lots of sex, preferably with someone you love. Is an explanation necessary? In a 2000 study of a sample of 900 women in Texas, no fewer than five well-respected researchers (including Daniel Kahneman) showed that sex is the primary contributor to happiness. (As an aside, meeting with your boss and commuting to work were at the bottom of the list.)
4. Invest in your relationships. Few factors, if any, have as strong an influence on your happiness as the ability to share both your joys and sorrows with a friend. In fact, sex, friendship, and to a certain extent marriage are exempt from hedonistic adaptation. We adapt more easily to things money can buy than things that cannot be acquired by money, like relationships.

5. Give your body the rest that it needs. Happy people are more active, but are also more vigilant about getting adequate rest. A sleep deficit leads to fatigue, loss of concentration, and depression.

6. Take charge of your time. Happy people feel that they control how they spend their time. Reassess your goals on a daily basis. When people attain their goals, they feel good about themselves. At the same time, it is important to remember that we have a tendency to overestimate how much we can accomplish in a given day and at the same time to underestimate what we can accomplish in a given year.

7. Look for a job that allows you to use your talents. The happiest people are those who can get into a state of "flow" – they are drawn into an activity that challenges them without overwhelming them. "Luxury" experiences, such as a cruise, are less likely to bring about "flow" than are gardening or spending time with friends.

8. Turn off the television. Studies show that as our life expectancy increases, most of us spend more time in front of the TV than we do at the office. The trouble with TV is that even though we choose the channel, we don't get to choose what we watch (loss of control). Characters on television are richer and better-looking than we are (the inevitable comparisons leave us frustrated), and the experience of watching TV is not usually shared with family and friends, whose contribution to happiness is so much more significant.

9. Be grateful. People who stop to appreciate their blessings – health, education, friends, family, freedom, sensory perception, a place to live – experience higher degrees of happiness.

10. Reach out and help others. While it is true that happiness strengthens our desire to help others, it is no less true that altruism leads to greater happiness. Find a social cause that resonates with you, and your life will be more meaningful.

Don't pursue happiness as an end in itself. Savor the moment. Because we don't really know what makes us happy, the quest for happiness per se is guaranteed to fail. Moreover, those people who try to attain happiness see all their activities as a means to an end, rather than appreciating them for what they are.

And always remember: success is achieving what you want. Happiness is wanting what you have.

ᯥ

The Bottom Line

On March 23, 1912, Robert Falcon Scott wrote his final words: "It seems a pity, but I do not think I can write more... Had we lived I should have had a tale to tell of the hardihood, endurance and courage of my companions which would have stirred the heart of every Englishman. These rough notes and our dead bodies must tell the tale..."

In the summer of 1911, Captain Scott, a British Royal Navy officer and experienced Antarctic explorer, led an English expedition in the so-called "Race to the South Pole." He set out on the grueling trek with ponies to carry the cargo, motor-powered sleighs and self-confidence that remained undeterred even when at last he reached his destination only to find a Norwegian flag fluttering over the southernmost point, planted in the snow by Roald Amundsen one month ahead of him.

Heartbroken, Scott journeyed back to the point of departure in particularly cruel weather. His final words were written a mere twelve miles from the supplies he had left at the outset. Had he reached them he could have told his story himself. His body and those of his four comrades were discovered by a search party eight months later, frozen in their sleeping bags.

Upon hearing the terrible news, England wrapped itself in deep mourning. Scott was declared a national hero, schools were named for him and his family secured its place in the nation's heart in a very moving ceremony conducted according to the best of British tradition.

Only fifty years later did people begin asking important questions: Were the ponies that sank into the deep snow at the outset of the trip the appropriate answer to Amundsen's trained sled dogs? Why did Scott carry with him more than sixty pounds of South Pole rock samples that hampered his team's movement? Was the size of the team optimal? Was this really only a case of bad luck?

Sir Ranulph Fiennes, Scott's biographer and a polar explorer in his own right, offers an interesting viewpoint on the subject. Fiennes believes that the criteria by which Scott was judged at the beginning of the twentieth century, when Britain was still an empire and a scientific research expedition was still part of national identity, are completely different to the criteria established in later years. Therefore, the test of time rendered pointless the deaths of Scott and his comrades, as recorded pathetically in the journals left behind in the snow.

As support for this observation – that success should be measured by changing criteria, according to the changing times – it is worthwhile recounting the story of Ernest Shackleton, another polar explorer and contemporary of Scott's. In 1914 Shackleton led an expedition of twenty-eight men across Antarctica, considered at the time to be the last remaining exploration challenge in that part of the world. Shackleton's ship became trapped in the ice and his crew was forced to abandon ship. At the height of the journey, Shackleton led his men to refuge on Elephant

Island before heading across 800 miles of open Antarctic Ocean to South Georgia Island with five other men in a rickety lifeboat. All twenty-eight men on *Endurance* survived their ordeal after spending twenty-two months in the Antarctic – even those whom Shackleton deemed unworthy of the royal citation they received upon return. The *Endurance* expedition became a landmark in leadership, determination and…endurance.

But this successful expedition had been preceded by an earlier one, in 1907, in which Shackleton had tried to conquer the South Pole. He turned back only 112 miles from his goal when he understood that he was insufficiently equipped to ensure the crew's safe return. That time as well, Shackleton did not lose a single man. Although he did not reach the Pole in 1907 and did not cross Antarctica in 1914, Shackleton has only become more solidly ensconced in the pantheon of British heroes. One book published a few years ago (from among many penned about the expedition), investigates the outstanding managerial principles employed by Shackleton during his expeditions.

The question, therefore, that needs to be asked, is: Over the course of time, what has brought about the dramatic differences in the way these two polar explorers – Scott and Shackleton, who were both revered in their own lifetimes – are perceived today?

It was World War II that caused the British to reassess their definition of success. While heroic sacrifice and representing the nation with honor were the norm at the beginning of the century, they later gave way to a more complex notion that took into consideration conditions, motives and, most especially, reasoned discretion in assessing risks, making these central factors in the process of anointing heroes. Thus, Scott failed to live up to the new standards while Shackleton embodied them.

Nature has its own simple answers with regards to success: it is all summed up in survival and reproduction. The queen bee, for example, flies at a height that can be matched by only the best-equipped male in the hive. Thus, the queen ensures that her offspring will be blessed with the very best genes. If no male succeeds in impregnating the queen, nature interprets the failure as a lack of males in the vicinity and causes males to hatch from all the eggs. However, the defining difference between humans and animals is culture, the outcome of our ability to think and record our thoughts. Indeed, as the story of Scott and Shackleton proves, the bottom line changes with time and with the cultural context. These days it has come full circle and shrunk to a definition reminiscent of Mother Nature's own evolutionary principles. According to cultural edicts of today, the bottom line has become the absolute criterion for success. This is due in large part – whether or not we wish to admit it – to the centrality of competitive sports in our lives and in the media since the 1980s, and its impact on the language of business.

In the language of sport, victory is not the most important thing – it is the only thing. Effort and luck play no part in the equation. In every year in which the Olympic Games are played, cries of "Go for the gold" can be heard in conference rooms and gatherings. The sad truth is that elite athletes in the individual sports are lone wolves who have long since given up on having any kind of social life in favor of obsessive training in battle-like conditions. Tiger Woods, the best of the world's golfing elite for the past few years, is an irrepressible perfectionist who insists on making his own bed in every hotel upon arrival and knows a week in advance what he will be wearing on a given day. Teamwork is the last thing that he and other excellent individual athletes like him promote. In fact, the main danger in adopting the mores of sport culture as the bottom line is that along with the very positive values of sport come simplistic thinking and over-emphasis on the world as a place primarily for competition.

Businesses that adopt the language of sport primarily miss out on the lesson concealed in failure. For people who wish to succeed, there is more information that can be derived from failures than from success stories. Failures are essential for personal growth and development. The modern bottom line, the ultimate shortcut for a culture drowning in numbers and information, completely misses out on the importance of the process as a basis for analysis. Analysis of process would enable the taking of steps toward making necessary improvements and ensuring the appropriate "result" in the future. Instead of the process, the bottom line adopts the result of the present as the crux of the matter and the sole indicator of future outcomes.

But the main disadvantage of the sport-influenced bottom line prevalent in the business world is the absolute disregard for the element of chance. We would like to believe that our success is based on our abilities and hard work, but there are many talented people who work hard and still do not succeed. Paul Getty cleverly related to this missing element in his answer when questioned on how to succeed and get rich: "Rise early, work hard, strike oil."

෴

Fish Tales

The Japanese are mad about fresh fish. As a result, the amount of fish in the waters around Japan has steadily decreased. In order to give the Japanese people the fish they love so dearly, the fisheries came up with a plan. They would build bigger and better fishing boats that could travel further away from shore.

There was, however, a snag: The further out the fishermen sailed, the longer it took them to return to the mainland. If the return trip was more than a couple of days, the fish, by definition, would no longer be fresh. This was not what the Japanese had in mind.

And so the fisheries came up with a new solution: they would install industrial-sized freezers on their boats. Now that the fishermen could flash-freeze their fish, they would be able to travel greater distances and stay at sea for longer periods of time. But no matter how quickly the fish were frozen, they didn't taste like fresh fish, and the Japanese could tell the difference. The frozen fish sold at a much lower price.

The fishery executives pondered this problem for some time before coming up with a new idea. The boats would be equipped with giant fish tanks. As soon as the fish were caught they would be tossed into the tank. They would thrash around for awhile, fin-to-fin; then they would stop. They would return to Japan tired and listless, but alive.

To the fishermen's dismay, the discriminating palates of the Japanese could still taste the difference. Because they hadn't moved around for days, the fish didn't taste fresh, and the Japanese, of course, preferred the fresh fish over the sluggish fish.

Imagine that at this point in the story you are hired by the Japanese fishing industry as their consultant. What would you advise them to do?

Here's how the problem was finally solved. In order to keep the fish fresh, the fisheries would continue to install tanks in each boat, with one major difference: this time, each tank came with a shark. At the price of losing a few unfortunate fish to the shark, the rest of them would be "on their toes" and in constant movement to avoid being devoured and as a result would reach the shore fresh and in excellent health. The challenge would do them good.

This story, which was first told in the 1950s, has been repeated countless times since then. It is told by university presidents who want to inspire their incoming freshmen, basketball coaches on the eve of a big game, and ice cream makers gearing up for winter. Whoever tells the story usually mentions L. Ron Hubbard, the writer and founder of Scientology. It was Hubbard who said, "Man thrives, oddly enough, only in the presence of a challenging environment."

Is this a true story? The newsletter "The Traveler," in its article on sight-seeing in Tokyo, lists the fish market as one of the essential sites. For tourists visiting the marketplace, the guide recommends the restaurant "Edu-Jin," in which the diner is invited to select his own dinner from the fish swimming around in the tank. It goes on to point out that the small shark swimming alongside them is not on the menu. This should put to rest any doubts about the story's veracity.

Whether or not this story is entirely true, it is a perfect allegory for our Western culture of materialism. Getting everything you want – a suitable partner, a good job, the erasure of all your debts – can squelch your ambition, make you complacent, and worst of all, keep you from aspiring to anything.

Challenge – the psychological key to our personal development – is the buzzword of today's consumer culture, a culture whose contribution to humanity remains to be seen. According to this theory, thinking about all the challenges that lie ahead infuse you with energy; when you are striving to find new solutions, you are fully alive. But don't bask in your success. Instead, as soon as you've overcome one challenge, you should set your goal on an even bigger one. In other words, put a shark in your tank and see how far you can swim.

In the history of humankind, the manic pace of our lives today is a relatively new phenomenon. Its origins can be traced back to the eighteenth century and the Age of Enlightenment, coupled with the Industrial Revolution. Its principal spokesman was the philosopher and economist Adam Smith. In his landmark book *The Wealth of Nations*, Smith argued that production has only one goal, and that is to be consumed. Clearly, humanity has undergone a momentous change since Aristotle's assertion that without leisure, there could be no action. In 1935, another prominent philosopher, Sir Bertrand Russell, published a collection of his articles entitled *In Praise of Idleness*.

The book could easily have been called *In Praise of Individualism*. The primary role of our culture, claimed Russell, is to distract us from the most important issue: our inevitable death. When we accelerate our pace of life, we can ignore our spiritual turmoil. Individualism is the true antidote to conformity, which leads us to put so many sharks in our tanks.

In the seventy years since the publication of Russell's book, we have succeeded in making our lives even more frenetic. This is why Carl Honore's latest book, *In Praise of Slowness*, is like a breath of fresh air. Honore, a Canadian journalist who lives in London, believes that the relentless pace of our society has failed to provide us with a healthy and satisfying life. He gives some chilling examples of how our compulsive lifestyle has tainted our food, our cities, our work, our leisure, and even the act of love itself. Honore contrasts this bleak picture with other cultures around the world, whose slower-paced lives comprise fewer challenges and more leisure time.

The website www.slowdownnow.com, which promotes a slower pace of life, offers the unhurried reader a selection of stories and essays about the slower side of life. A description of the English afternoon tea ceremony appears alongside a philosophical meditation on the difficulty of waking up in the morning. One section of the site is dedicated to famous writers and thinkers, like the mathematician and philosopher Blaise Pascal, who in 1650 wrote that "All men's miseries derive from not being able to sit in a quiet room alone." Or Marcel Proust, whose illness, real or imagined, kept him bedridden for ten years. One of his most brilliant passages is a description of a man lying in bed and trying to fall back asleep, a description that takes up no fewer than 17 pages.

To conclude, if we go back to our opening story of the fish: the challenge does not prolong the lives of the fish, even if it does keep them fresh. Within a short time, they will all have died anyway, whether in the jaws of the shark or under the knife of the great sushi chef in the sky.

Snowflakes and Success

It is said that no two snowflakes are alike. If we recall that the number of possible combinations that form a snowflake is finite, albeit very large, we will find yet another example of our inability to differentiate between "infinite" and "very large."

A snowflake is an agglomeration of ice crystals that can appear as a simple hexagon formed from a single ice crystal all the way up to a highly complex star shape. Snowflakes that fall from the sky are among the more complex forms.

A little Science 101: Careful investigation of the single water molecule that comprises an ice crystal reveals that one in five thousand of these molecules contains an unusual hydrogen atom in whose nucleus there is a single proton and – contrary to the norm – a neutron. These isotopes of hydrogen are scattered through the entire crystal, and since a single ice crystal can contain 10^{18} water molecules, the chance that two crystals will be alike is infinitesimal. The random nature of the crystal's growth merely reinforces the dimensions of its complexity. By way of example, the number of different ice crystals that could result from such aggregations, based on the fifteen parameters for characterizing an ice crystal, would be more than a trillion.

Humans are no less complex than snowflakes, so it can be safely stated that we will not find two people completely identical in the entire universe. But what if we were to reduce our search to the population of businesspeople, and even further to businesspeople who have succeeded? Will we then be able to come up with two identical success stories?

In order to remain in the realm of snowflakes, I have decided to name fifteen parameters that characterize, in differing dosages, most success stories I know of: grit, determination, optimism, patience, integrity, individualism, ability to delegate authority, talent, self-discipline, quantitative thinking, sociability, good judgment of character, creativity, intuition and charisma. I could have added additional variables but this list is enough to determine that the chance that two successful businesspeople will share an identical combination of characteristics from this list is about the same as finding two identical snowflakes: practically nil.

The thousands of books that record the life stories and credentials of successful entrepreneurs prove again and again that there are no two identical success stories and that the path to success is variegated and multifaceted, even if we ignore the element of luck that appears in many of those stories.

Nonetheless, it is hard to relinquish the hope of discovering the one characteristic, perhaps joined with another, that determines the greatest chance for success. Is it possible to find a common denominator among most success stories? A series of research studies carried out by Angela Duckworth and Martin Seligman at the University of Pennsylvania bring new light to the subject. By analyzing a large number of success stories and carrying out specially-designed experiments, Duckworth and Seligman discovered that natural talent is likely to play only a minor role in achieving success. Their opinion is that determination, diligence and patience are the keys to success in school, at work, and in the business world. Those characteristics aid us in dealing with the unavoidable mishaps and impediments that occur in every attempt to realize long-term plans.

Intelligence and determination are two completely independent characteristics. Both increase the chance of success, but the more talented among us do not necessarily possess more determination than the untalented. Further, intelligence is, according to the researchers, responsible in only 25% of success stories.

In a different study mentioned in the December 2005 issue of Psychology Today, it was shown that parents who praised their children's natural aptitudes (instead of their efforts) actually harmed their ability to deal with failure. Those children praised for the efforts they have invested (and not their aptitudes) behaved in the face of failure as if they had been recharged, while the former experienced a lack of confidence in their own talents when dealing with failure.

Indeed, experts speak often of the "ten-year rule." According to this notion, it takes at least a decade (!) of hard work to succeed in any enterprise or job, from managing a children's clothing store to screenwriting. The ability to face the challenging impediments and surprises that arise is what ultimately determines success.

We are socially conditioned to think that natural aptitude is the key to success. But the success stories with which I am familiar, as well as scientific research, prove that the true determining factor is a mix of passion, determination, resilience and diligence. It was worth waiting; in a world of instant gratification, patience has its virtue.

Working Out with Polar Bears

How many times do you press the "snooze" button on your alarm clock and go back to sleep? When you try to control your feelings, can other people still read you like an open book? When your energy level is low, do you make it to the gym anyway?

We all have an intuitive sense of our own level of self-discipline. We can exercise an admirable degree of self-control when it comes to working hard. However, in the face of temptation (whether to put off what is required of us until tomorrow, or succumb to drinking, smoking or gambling), all our best intentions fade away.

Self-discipline can be measured, as was demonstrated by psychologist Walter Mischel's landmark study from the early1970s. Mischel gathered a group of four-year-olds in a room with a bowl of marshmallows and a bell; then he left. If a child rang the bell, the psychologist would go back into the room and reward that child with a marshmallow. However, if a child waited patiently for Mischel to return to the room on his own, he or she would receive two marshmallows.

In the video recording of the experiment, we witness the heart-wrenching efforts of the toddlers to exercise self-restraint and receive the extra treat. Some of the kids covered their eyes, others rested their heads on their arms in a futile attempt to fall asleep, still others talked, and even sang, to themselves. Nonetheless, their levels of self-discipline varied greatly. Some of the kids caved in almost immediately, while others were able to wait the full fifteen minutes – an eternity, to a pre-schooler – before the psychologist returned.

Years later, in a follow-up study, the scientists learned something interesting, though not surprising. Apparently, those children who had controlled themselves in the initial experiment had grown up to be self-disciplined adults, willing to delay their gratification in order to achieve a long-term goal. They were socially well-adjusted, and their frustration threshold was quite high. On the other hand, the kids who weren't able to wait for that second marshmallow had gone on to become stubborn, anxious, and indecisive adults.

As a rule, children – especially small children – are not good at self-control. The part of the brain that is responsible for self-discipline does not fully develop until a person's early twenties. The question is, can we manipulate the normal pattern of childhood development in such an important area?

The good news is that a series of studies confirms that indeed, we can strengthen our self-discipline and resolve by practicing restraint and self-control, just as you strengthen a muscle through exercise. Unfortunately, much like physical exercise, you cannot sustain this strength for an unlimited period of time. Eventually, you get run down.

After a long day at work, our self-discipline muscle is weak, and the tactics that we relied on earlier fail us. This is when we eat too much junk food or yell at our spouse.

A 2007 study that was published in the Journal of Consumer Research attests to this phenomenon. A group of American high school students was asked to write down their stream-of-consciousness thoughts for several minutes. The only stipulation was that they were not allowed to think about polar bears. Another group was given the same assignment, but with no limitations. As an incentive, each participant was given a small sum of money to put towards a limited selection of products. The study showed that those students who were asked to refrain from thinking about polar bears ended up spending a lot more money than their unrestricted counterparts.

According to the researcher, this study proves that self-discipline is, in fact, a limited resource. In other words, the students in the first group were running low on self-control. Their supply had dwindled. These students displayed a low level of self-discipline, a stronger desire to buy things, and a willingness to spend more money than they anticipated they would have before the experiment.

In another study, led by Baba Shiv and Alexander Fedorikhin at Stanford University in 1999, one group of subjects was asked to remember a two-digit number, while the other group was asked to remember a seven-digit number. As the subjects were being escorted to another part of the building, they passed a table with chocolate cake and fruit salad. Sixty-three percent of the people in the first group – the two-digit group – chose the fruit salad, as opposed to 41% of the seven-digit group. Having to remember five additional numbers was enough of an effort to deplete their supply of self-control.

The subjects who had to remember the extra numbers had used up more mental energy than those with the simpler task. As we have demonstrated, mental energy is a limited resource, and the people who put more energy towards the first goal (remembering the extra digits) had less energy left over for the second goal (resisting temptation). In fact, the area of the brain that is responsible for short-term memory is located in the front of the brain, right next to the area responsible for self-discipline. The task of remembering numbers uses the same neurons that, if they were available, would help us make a responsible choice about what, and how much, to eat.

Similar findings were generated in another diet-related study. Early in the day, subjects were offered a breakfast cereal. Later that day, they were invited to take part in an ice cream tasting. The group that had exercised self-restraint that morning ate a lot more than those who hadn't been able to resist the snack. Moreover, when they were given a challenging mathematical problem to solve, those who had avoided the snack gave up 40% earlier. Apparently, they had used up their daily ration of self-discipline earlier that morning, and couldn't muster up the inner strength to resist other temptations – in this case, the temptation to give up on the math problem before solving it.

All the research points to the same conclusion: after devoting all of one's self-discipline to a particular task, it is very hard to exercise the same degree of control on another, unrelated, task. After dealing with a challenging situation that demands restraint and self-discipline, we run out of willpower.

If self-discipline is, in fact, a muscle, the most important lesson to be learned is that we have to choose our battles very carefully. Instead of trying to excel all the time, we should reserve our determination for when it really matters. And if you're on a diet, cut yourself some slack, and let yourself think about polar bears.

Dice from Heaven

May 30th, 1867, the wedding day of Princess Maria del Poso and Duke Amadeu, the son of the king of Italy, was not the happiest day in the lives of many of those involved. The wardrobe mistress hanged herself, the palace gatekeeper slit his own throat, the officer administering the service was sun-struck and collapsed, one of the ushers shot himself and the manager of the local train station (Turin) was run over by the honeymoon carriage. From every other point of view, all ran smoothly.

Was it an exceptionally bizarre coincidence or simply bad luck, such that would haunt the couple for the remainder of their lives? Are coincidences God's way of remaining anonymous, or, as Darwin claimed, nature's way of manifesting itself?

Well, the answer depends on whom you ask. A statistician, for one, would try to find a possible explanation for the events at hand by estimating the probability of unrequited love between some of the individuals involved, as well as the probability of being involved in a train accident (one to half-a-million) and in general, claim that such a one-in-a-million affair in a country with a population of several millions, is an ordinary daily occurrence.

Despite the alluring logic of such an attitude, it fails to provide us with an adequate explanation to the charm of coincidences, especially those in which we are involved personally.

Do we not feel a magical sensation when we think of someone just as the phone rings and we hear their voice on the other line? We tend to view such events as more than simple coincidences. For our very existence is a result of a unique coincidence in which certain chemical chains combined to create life, and despite the fact that human evolution has been a series of random gene mutations – our desperate yearning to give our life a meaning beyond random luck arises whenever coincidences happen to us. "If we were indeed chosen by Fate to star in a coincidence," we say, "then the world is probably less threatening and we are not as small and insignificant."

How could we explain the fact that – a hundred years after Einstein proclaimed that "God does not play with dice," and after a series of scientific discoveries that shaped significantly our understanding of the world – 40% of all scientists specializing in exact and natural sciences still testify to their belief in a higher power?

Coincidences play a central role in reinforcing such belief. When we experience a unique coincidence, the statistical, rational explanation is rejected in favor of the consolation the realms of guidance and supervision can provide – the touch of a higher power leaving its orderly mark on the chaos of our troubled lives.

Profound statistical comprehension is needed to separate the fantastic and the real from a mathematical point of view. But nature, grasping to protect us, has made us statistically blind. We become prepared to face any existential threat disregarding the probability of its occurrence. Who could have imagined that the chance of dying in an airplane accident is forty times smaller than the chance of choking while dining?

Writer Paul Auster believes that we are shaped by the powers of coincidences. Schopenhauer claimed that the importance of coincidences lies in the fact that they are tailor-made to fit the individual experiencing them. Psychologist Carl Jung took a further step in this direction when he coined the term "Synchronistic Occurrence." His definition broadens the realm of the coincidence by incorporating the human experience, necessarily private, in the face of incidental events. A synchronistic occurrence brings together the objective outside world of the coincidence with the subjective inner world of the protagonist.

A large proportion of the significant synchronistic occurrences in one's life have to do with incidental encounters with the right person at the right moment or at a time of atypical emotional openness. At such times, said Jung, it is important to be mindful of the emotive experience and to the emotion that arises, because these may present us with valuable insights. Similar to the growth potential that arises from interpreting our dreams, the synchronistic occurrence represents the potential of a dream – that what may have been dreamt by someone other than ourselves could affect similar changes.

How unfortunate that our business culture limits such potential, since the analytical statistician still enjoys the upper hand over the emotional dream interpreter.

Our work environment and our easy access to information have opened us to coincidences vastly greater than those our parents were exposed to. Will we be able to see the opportunity these represent for our potential to grow?

We could discuss this matter if we were to bump into one another on the street, say, a short while after you finish reading this chapter.

DOING IT YOUR OWN WAY

◦◦

"It is not worth an intelligent man's time to be in the majority.
By definition, there are already enough people to do that."
- G. H. Hardy, British mathematician (1877-1947)

Eulogy

One of the central challenges faced by the alchemists of the business world is the attempt at deciphering the personality code of the successful entrepreneur. If only we were able to assess the person sitting across from us as equipped with the characteristics of the successful entrepreneur, we would invest our money or work in tandem with him or her, finding one way or another of putting this advance information to good use.

Over the course of my twenty years as an investor, and, more specifically as a venture capital investor, I have interviewed hundreds of entrepreneurs. I have always been on the lookout for the winning personality, convinced that it would be easier to make a manager out of a winner than trying to make a winner out of even an experienced manager. Especially in venture capital, the equation is simple: the winners win, for themselves and for us.

Early on I learned that several of the myths surrounding entrepreneurs are not necessarily a reflection of reality. The average entrepreneur is thirty-five years old, and not in his/her twenties; average in intelligence (not a genius); and quite often has decided not to pursue a degree in business administration. The successful entrepreneur's résumé will most likely include ten years of work at established companies, often even only one company for the duration.

The makeup of each entrepreneur is different from the next one, and successful entrepreneurs do not come from the same mold. Still, profiling successful entrepreneurs reveals that most share a common characteristic that is their chief motivation. Unsurprisingly, the heat source for the motivating factor is also shared by most successful entrepreneurs.

These entrepreneurs are not motivated, as is commonly believed, by the desire to become rich. Anyone who has spent enough time in investments knows to treat an entrepreneur solely interested in financial gain like the plague. The desirable entrepreneur, on the other hand, is mainly motivated by a sense of mission, and he aspires wholeheartedly to make his mark by way of his financial prowess, a kind of footprint in the sand of the business world. Or, to paraphrase Napoleon – a political and economic entrepreneur par excellence – "Glory is fleeting but obscurity is forever."

"What would you like to have achieved by ten years from now?" That is one of the most frequently asked questions when interviewing entrepreneurs, as a means of assessing the level of the candidate's ambition via his or her personal and business vision. A cruder but more effective way of ascertaining the same information is "How would you like to be eulogized?" For those who fear the candidate will be so offended by the question that he will pick up and leave the room, stranding the interviewer alone with his morose thoughts, here is an alternative version: "Imagine that in another ten years, Forbes or Fortune will write a cover story about you. What would you like the headline to be?"

The answer to that challenging question can be categorized in one of two ways. The first includes such examples as "Incredibly successful John Jones has not compromised his values/lost his humility/forgotten his school chums" (select the most appropriate option). This represents the entrepreneur for whom prestige and honor are particularly important and whose entrepreneurial successes are meant to solidify his position in his reference group. The second category includes this type of answer: "John Jones succeeds wildly on his own road to success." This is the kind of entrepreneur who wishes to make his mark.

Let's be clear about this: both of these types of entrepreneurs are likely to deliver the goods. I personally have always favored the second type, since he/she is more efficient. While there is no underestimating the personality motivated by prestige and social standing, he/she can be fueled by an inefficient energy source: I contend that a contaminated ego is one of the principal obstacles in the business world. On the other hand, when a person is dying to make a mark, his compass will always point him in the right direction, helping him navigate toward his goal in the most efficient manner. He will not tarry for the purpose of feeding his need for respect and appreciation, which compromise efficiency.

Anyone who has spent even a little time among successful entrepreneurs knows that they are not satisfied with themselves and as a rule can be characterized by the disquiet that is part and parcel of people who have absolutely no choice but to prove themselves. The successful entrepreneur is – how can this be expressed gently? – a bit neurotic. Obsessive behavior, a need to control, and perfectionism are just a few of the symptoms shared by many successful entrepreneurs, and these apparently derive in no small measure from the existential insecurity that attaches itself to an entrepreneur like a shadow from an early age. The reasons for this insecurity are varied: rejection in childhood, lack of emotional warmth from one or both parents, social ostracism or some other emotional wound. We all carry some of that inside, but the entrepreneur more so.

The successful entrepreneur is determined to heal that early wound by means of success in business that he unconsciously believes will serve as a balm to his aching soul. Obviously, an emotional scar of major proportions is liable to render an entrepreneur powerless or incapable of handling the issues that crop up in business, so that in place of the necessary dollop of neurosis we are faced with a toxic mélange of personality traits that can spoil the entire entrepreneurial stew.

Optimism is another trait that fuels the entrepreneurial engine and acts as a counterbalance to insecurity; without it, the entrepreneur doesn't have a prayer. Optimism is the fundamental feeling that renders the world as a place rich with opportunities that the entrepreneur can one day make use of for his own needs. As Churchill said, it is optimism that enables the entrepreneur to march confidently from failure to failure without losing even a bit of the enthusiasm that characterizes him. Optimism is also what enables him to flourish when a proper assessment would cause him to steer clear of an opportunity altogether. Here, too, as with insecurity, everything depends on the amount, the dosage.

There is a delicate balance in being the sufficiently neurotic entrepreneur capable of properly assessing reality. Excessive optimism is liable to wreak havoc on the ability to make proper judgments and cause an entrepreneur to ignore the warning signs that most failing enterprises emit at an early enough stage to be caught in time.

Fortunately for those who interview entrepreneurs, optimism is an easily identifiable trait, and the candidate's own testimony with regards to optimism is quite reliable. In this matter I tend to pose questions to potential entrepreneurs about traumas in their lives, mainly painful failures and mistaken choices. Surprisingly, the optimistic entrepreneur does not delve deeply into these questions. For him, the chain of events that comprise his life serve as an ongoing process of personal and professional development. The optimistic entrepreneur does not recognize the exceptional importance of some event or decision since all of them have aided him in finding the path to his own personal footprint in the sand.

But what about money? How does money connect to all this? For the entrepreneur it is a byproduct. Its importance lies in the fact that it is the only means for objectively measuring success, or, if you wish, the depth of the footprint one leaves behind.

∽

Murder on the Investment Committee

A bizarre crime that took place in New York one night in 1964 inspired one of the most important psychological studies of the twentieth century.

That night after work, Kitty Genovese returned to her home in Queens. An unknown assailant, later identified as Winston Moseley, stabbed her in the back and again later in the stomach. At the sound of her screams, lights went on in the nearby buildings but not a single resident of the neighborhood took action. Little by little the lights went out and the assailant, who was already on the way to his car, returned to finish the murder. The crime took place over a period of thirty-five minutes; the New York Times claimed that thirty-eight witnesses had watched from their windows as the young woman fought for her life but did not raise a finger to help her.

Like many other New Yorkers, John Darley of New York University and Bibb Latane of Columbia University followed the description of the murder and the subsequent responses by readers of the Times with horror. As social psychologists, they felt that the explanation for the questionable behavior of bystanders to a terrible crime had a lot more to with the circumstances than with the personalities of the onlookers.

In an experiment planned by Darley and Latane, a naive subject was placed in a room and told that he was to talk about normal stress problems with other students who were similarly in isolated rooms, ostensibly to preserve anonymity. Actually, all the other students were on tape. One of the other students suffers an epileptic seizure and calls for help. It was found that if the subject of the experiment was convinced that others could hear the victim of the seizure from their own rooms, he would be less likely to take action, much as Kitty Genovese's neighbors failed to heed her cries for help. Fully two-thirds of those subjects tested made no effort to assist the person having a seizure, while 85% who believed themselves to be the only person hearing the seizure responded.

The close correlation between the percentage of people who rush to help and the size of the group led the researchers to coin a new term: Shared Responsibility. The experiment showed that the larger the number of witnesses, the less responsibility each bystander feels. This phenomenon apparently stems from social factors that cause the individual to abstain from taking action and assuming responsibility that could potentially embarrass him later on ("Perhaps it was just a lover's quarrel...").

Is it possible that an investment committee – the very heart of the decision-making system of any institution dealing with investments – might be exposed to the Shared Responsibility phenomenon as well? The large body of scientific material gathered until now supports the supposition that group decisions are prone to disaster.

The main advantage of the group over the individual is the greater pool of knowledge and skills available to the group. However, in practice it is clear that groups are deficient when it comes to their ability to float that knowledge and those skills between its members; instead, they tend to discuss shared information (information known by all group members) more than unshared information. Researches have named this phenomenon the Hidden Profile.

In a well-known study of the Hidden Profile conducted by Dennis Stewart and Gary Stasser, different groups of three people were asked to select the most suitable candidate for the position of marketing director. The researchers compiled three résumés for the three candidates, which included fifteen different bits of information for each candidate. One candidate's résumé stood out, was in fact nearly perfect for the job. Each member of the test group received only a portion of the information, though all the relevant information could be found amongst the three group members. If the group members were able to share their information successfully, they would immediately identify the preferred candidate.

However, 90% of the groups that participated in the experiment failed to share the necessary information. They tended not to bring up negative information about candidates who showed real promise or positive information about those who were deemed less suitable. This phenomenon naturally favored consensus over the possibility of additional complexity or fruitful discussion. It repeats itself and is confirmed in other studies and leads to skewed discussion that does not make best use of the group. The discussion focuses on information known to all the group members, in spite of the fact that the group would profit from receiving information that its members do not already share. In a skewed discussion, participants prefer to discuss only that information which supports the central idea of the group. Studies show that when the group nears consensus, there is a rise in the frequency of discussing only that information which supports the consensus. Further, one study reveals, those group members who share data that confirm the group's viewpoint are perceived as talented and more credible both in the eyes of the group and in their own eyes. This phenomenon is referred to, not surprisingly, as Mutual Reinforcement.

The following is a list of ten rules for improving the sharing of information among committee members as gleaned from the more important research studies carried out in recent years:

- Longer discussions lead to greater sharing of information.
- If the participants tend to attribute expertise to other members of the discussion they will cause those perceived as experts to share more information.
- If the participants are requested to adopt a critical attitude, more information will be shared among the participants.
- Information that is negative and kept hidden is more likely to be disseminated among committee members than positive information.
- Differences of opinion from before the discussion lead to a greater sharing of information.
- A discussion among peers in an organization is more effective than among superiors and inferiors, since the presence of a hierarchy inhibits the sharing of information.

- When members of the committee are requested to document information, more of it is shared among group members.
- The ranking of options leads to a greater dissemination of information.
- If committee members know that they are expected to share information and not just make decisions, more information is indeed shared.
- Pictures serve as better reminders than words.

If you find it difficult to adopt the scientific wisdom of this list, you can always follow the advice of those who believe that in order for a committee to be effective in the decision-making process it should comprise three members only, of whom two will conveniently be absent for the discussion itself.

The reason for failing to share information brings us back to the discovery made by Darley and Latane with regards to the social component of our behavior. We are liable to silence our voices as witnesses to a murder or as members of an investment committee if we fear the way others will perceive us. The "others" do not, for some reason, include the many investors who are meant to be served by the investment committee.

The Riddle of Hungarian Applause

In March 2006 the heads of the Budapest Spring Festival were faced with the nightmare of orchestral managers of every generation: the unusually warm weather brought not only a large number of tourists but a virus that struck down the two main performers as well – the conductor and the solo pianist. Alexander Sladkovsky, principal conductor of the Saint Petersburg Capella Symphony Orchestra and well known to the festival organizers, was asked to step in as conductor. Entrusting the Budapest Philharmonic's debut performance of Chopin's Concerto No. 1 for Piano to an Italian pianist by the name of Pietro De Maria was more daring.

The Budapest Spring Festival has a particularly successful history of last-minute replacement of musicians, and the 2006 festival was no exception. The audience was very appreciative of the young pianist's exciting performance and of the conductor's inspiring rendition of Tchaikovsky's Symphony No. 2, which brought the evening to a close. The applause continued for no less than twelve minutes, and this is of interest to us.

In Hungary and other countries of Eastern Europe, an audience expresses appreciation for a good performance by the strength and nature of its applause. The initial thunder often turns into synchronized clapping, which has a well-defined pattern: strong incoherent clapping at the outset is followed by a relatively sudden synchronization process, after which everybody claps simultaneously and periodically. This spontaneous synchronization can disappear and reappear several times during the applause, or, as in the case of the Budapest Spring Festival of 2006, dozens of times.

The ability of hundreds of members of an audience to coordinate their applause is a known phenomenon; so, too, is the fact that from the moment it manages this feat, an audience needs relatively little effort to maintain the beat. So why does the audience prefer instead to revert to the chaos that characterizes the onset of the process, repeating it again and again?

Zoltán Néda, a Romanian professor of theoretical physics first exposed to the phenomenon at the end of a performance of Ionesco's The Bald-Headed Singer in Hungary, was determined to solve the riddle. Together with Albert-László Barabási of the University of Notre Dame and several other colleagues, Néda conducted a study that is clearly one of the oddest in the history of physics.

The researchers probably envisioned flocks of migrating birds flying in pattern, schools of thousands of fish moving as a single entity or the synchronized flashing of Southeast Asian fireflies, which light up the night in flashes that can be seen for miles. Mathematicians call this phenomenon Global Oscillation, whereby crickets synchronize their chirping, pacemaker cells in the heart synchronize the contractions that pump 2.72 fluid ounces of blood through our bodies with each heartbeat, and women living together for long periods of time menstruate in a synchronized fashion.

A precondition for Global Oscillation is a low variance of the measured phenomena, in our case the applause of the audience.

After recording several theater and opera performances in Romania and Hungary, the researchers analyzed the results according to sound volume, noise intensity (volume divided by time) and average noise intensity.

They discovered that typically, after a few seconds of random clapping, a periodic signal of pronounced pikes develops. While synchronization increases the strength of the signal at the moment of the clapping, it surprisingly leads to a decrease in the average noise intensity in the room. Apparently, the conflicting desire of the audience to simultaneously increase the average noise intensity and maintain synchronization leads to the sequence of appearing and disappearing synchronized patterns.

So how do the researchers explain the strange behavior of the Eastern European audiences that zigzag between two types of hand-clapping? The human capacity for coordinating the sounds of individuals into a tribal chorus has clear evolutionary roots, providing a significant tool for survival against distant predators attempting to assess the size of their potential prey according to the level of noise it makes.

Everyone is familiar with the feeling we get from being part of a group – cheering on a sporting competition, taking part in a demonstration, watching the voting results with a crowd of people on Election Day. Researchers claim that the musical descendants of prehistoric man are torn between two conflicting desires. The first – primal, immediate – is the spontaneous wish of the audience to express its appreciation to the artists who have just performed for them. Quite naturally, this message grows clearer as the intensity of the sound increases. And that, the researchers found, is higher when the applause is random. The other is the desire to belong to the group and to gain another chance to listen to the artists. Friendly, rhythmic clapping carries this message, which is cultural in nature, most efficiently.

Accelerating the rhythm, which reflects the urgency of the audience's request, causes each individual member of the audience to applaud the artists at his own rate when the performers return to the stage.

The dynamic of Hungarian applause raises the question that faces society in general and business institutions in particular: Is the power of the institution concealed in the variation and uniqueness of every employee, or is it, in fact, in the common denominator that they share? Is an institution more efficient in reaching a common goal than the individuals that comprise it, even if the latter are more intense in expressing themselves? And in general, can an individual realize any cultural or economic goal without the aid of other individuals – partners, clients, employees, mentors and others?

Tennis star Althea Gibson, the first African-American woman to win at Wimbeldon (1955), had a simple answer to this question: "No matter what accomplishment you achieve, someone helps you."

∽

The Admiralty Regrets...

Walter Arnold was born on October 28th, 1909, with a fine membrane covering his face, a membrane that was easily removed by the skilled midwife. Echoing a widespread superstition of the time, she commented, "Anyone born with such a veil would never drown." And Petty Officer Stoker Mechanic Arnold never did. Not even when ninety-nine of his shipmates perished onboard His Majesty's Submarine *Thetis*, thirty years later.

Was Arnold saved because of his good fortune as the midwife prophesized at his birth? As we survey the events that took place during two stormy days, three months before the outbreak of the World War II, it appears that Arnold had something else beside good fortune going for him.

Thetis, a new T-model submarine, set out on its first voyage from Cammell Lairds Harbor on June 1st, 1939, carrying 103 men – crewmembers, dockworkers, and others – as was customary on first voyages, in total twice the allowable number.

The reasons for which the bow-cap of tube No. 5 was left wide open, in complete disregard of the directives, and are unknown to this very day. But we do know why Lt. Commander Bulos could not have known that the tube was bursting with water, before he opened the other bow-cap, the one leading into the submarine body. A drop of enamel from the brush of a dockworker was blocking a thin pipeline that served as a test cock, indicating whether there was water inside the tube. As a result, it seemed that the tube was dry while, in fact, it was filled with seawater waiting to break into the submarine. The opening of the tube bow-cap during a routine assessment consequently brought insurmountable amounts of water into the *Thetis*. The two front compartments were flooded. The vessel immediately sank to the bottom of Liverpool Bay, not far from the place where it had set sail.

The awful news stunned the nation. And yet hope rekindled when it became known that the stern of the submarine was in fact above water-surface. It seemed as if the only thing necessary was to breach the stern and allow oxygen in, thus permitting the rescue of the trapped crewmen.

Why did this scenario never take place? Why did the Admiralty not act with the vigor and urgency necessary to rescue its human resources?

"The Admiralty Regrets…," the opening line of the telegrams of condolence sent at the event of a loss of life in the navy, is the name of a fascinating book that traces the minute-by-minute development of this tragic affair: the catastrophes, the mistakes, and the indecision and awful apathy that characterized those meant to lead and organize the rescue operation.

The rescuing party first lost the co-ordinates of the submarine, then found them, lost them again, re-found them, and lost them once more. The above-water rescuing effort was delayed due to outdated technology and the need to hasten ships to the disaster area.

The Admiralty learned only afterward that the number of unfortunate passengers twice exceeded the norm. It assumed, mistakenly, that the oxygen would last for 36 hours, twice the amount of time it actually did.

Is it possible that the navy, on the verge of a second World War, preferred salvaging the submarine body to saving the lives of the men aboard it? For it seems that it would have been possible to rescue the men with relative ease – in exchange for the possible loss of the vessel.

At this point, two men escaped, cleverly utilizing the escape pod, thus floating to safety. A second rescue mission ended with the death of three other crewmembers, but not before the escape pod outlet opened into the submarine, creating a short circuit that fatally intensified the level of carbon dioxide.

The salvage pod turned into a death trap. The Lt. Commander desperately sought volunteers for another rescue mission. The plea was whispered from mouth-to-ear with choking breaths. Navy Stoker Arnold volunteered. He might have realized that waiting for the Admiralty rescue forces involved greater risk than the risk involved in attempting to save himself.

He and another volunteer arrived safely onto the deck of the rescue ship. He was then greeted by a doctor who immediately drugged him. It was the first step of many in a vast conspiracy to bury the evidence, for the Admiralty was desperate to conceal its failures.

In this book, the British Admiralty of the time epitomizes the characteristics of many bureaucratic organizations: inefficiency, internal struggles, ineptness, and a deficient list of priorities, one in which human life is not always at the top.

Navy Stoker Arnold clearly saw that if he took the initiative instead of waiting for his fleet commanders, he would gain his life.

Are you also trapped in your own submarine? Working under dense executives that are engaged in political intrigues, with an inadequate list of priorities that fails to see the welfare of employees as an overriding concern? Four out of a hundred escaped from the *Thetis*. Could you have been one of them?

෭ඏ

The Stock Market's Skirt

In the Fall of 2004, Canadian media artist Nancy Paterson exhibited an oddly-titled work, Stock Market's Skirt, which featured a mannequin dressed in a blue taffeta and black velvet party dress. Computer screens that flickered current stock quotes from the Toronto Stock Exchange were spread about. An additional screen analyzed the changing stock quotes and activated a hidden motor that caused the hem of the skirt to rise or fall according to whether the market itself was rising or falling.

The theory of the connection between the height of women's skirts and the performance of the stock market has been around for a while. The basic assumption is that hems rise with consumer confidence, and with it, the optimism of the stock market.

In fact, the theory does not stand up to scientific scrutiny, even though the data from certain periods present fascinating correlations. Thus, for example, the rise in the Dow Jones index in the summer of 1971 when hot pants were all the rage, or the welcome influence of miniskirts on the stock market in 1993. Still, this lightweight theory could never have struck a chord with so many people were it not for the fact that we feel that clothes play an important role in the business world.

Canadian sociologist Erving Goffman laid the philosophical groundwork for understanding this connection. In a book he published in 1959, *The Presentation of Self in Everyday Life*, Goffman imbues Shakespeare's statement that "All the world's a stage" with sociological content by claiming that our lives are a collection of encounters with other individuals or groups. In each of these encounters we play the role of the "performer," while others act as our "audience" and react to our "performance." According to this approach, our identity is defined by the sum total of our performances so that we have no single, clear identity. The self is an entity that changes with the nature of the performance and reacts differently to each audience. As long as we wrap our performance in the appropriate garb for a certain encounter, everything that lies beneath it – most notably, our personality – is less important.

If in fact it is possible to describe life as a series of encounters in each of which we carry out a different performance, then the business meeting should have its own special place. It is relatively short, the props are familiar to all involved, and in many cases it is a one-time performance. Under these circumstances, the importance of the clothes one wears becomes even more central. The right choice is likely to create the proper impression for this performance.

Indeed, when we are in the presence of people with whom we are not familiar, we try to assess certain aspects of their identities – their socioeconomic status, self-image, talents, even credibility – by the clothes they wear. This information is important for managing both the meeting and expectations with regards to the outcome. This is true both for the performer and the audience.

The reaction of the audience cannot be anticipated in advance. In a study of airport check-in agents working for various airlines, it was discovered that travelers in business suits were more likely to be upgraded. In contrast, sales personnel at high-end shops are difficult to deceive. They notice the quality of a person's watch or, especially, his or her shoes, and ignore other aspects of a customer's appearance. For them, there is a strong correlation between shabby shoes and customers who ask a lot of questions but do not, ultimately, make a purchase.

When we stand in front of the closet on the morning of an important meeting, we make an exceedingly meaningful decision with regards to our ability to manage our performance. We decide who it is we wish to be today. More than we really are? Less? Exactly who we really are? Someone else completely?

Take an example from about three thousand years ago: in one of the Bible's greatest encounters, David goes out to fight Goliath. Saul, fearful for David's safety, provides him with his own battledress and sword, places a copper helmet on his head and dresses him in armor. But David, uncomfortable in clothing that is not his own, removes it, preferring instead to meet Goliath with his walking stick, his shepherd's bag and his slingshot with five stones he has collected. That is the only way he can feel at ease. His clothing and his identity are not at odds, which would weaken him during battle. Intriguingly, in Biblical Hebrew the roots of the words "cloth" and "treason" are identical.

Goffman's work raises an important question: to what extent are we a single entity with a clear identity, or a structure with many faces? The answer may well be found in our closets. If the only thing hanging there is a dozen little black dresses of the same cut, that is the sign of a uniform, well-defined identity. Unless of course we are talking about a man, for whom a closet full of little black dresses would certainly be a sign of rebellion...

Six Degrees of Separation

In 1912, Frigyes Karinthy became the most famous author in Hungary with his book *That's the Way You Write*, a collection of poems and short stories written as literary parodies of the most famous voices of the literary world at that time. He was only twenty-five years old at the time. He published his forty-sixth book (!) in 1929, a collection of more than fifty stories, one of which, *Láncszemek* (*Chains*), raises the idea that one could reach every one of the 1.5 billion citizens of the earth (at that time) through no more than five connections.

Only forty years after *Chains* was published, Karinthy's literary insight received scientific backing. Professor Stanley Milgram, who became famous for a series of experiments that tested the moral aspects of obeying authority, offered a new way of investigating the issue, which he called The Small World Problem.

For the purposes of his study, carried out at Harvard University, Milgram selected two target people: one was the wife of a divinity student and the other a broker, both from the Boston area. He then randomly asked people in three different cities in the Midwest to send packages to one of these two people. The senders were given the name of the target person, his/her profession and general whereabouts. They were instructed to send the package via a personal acquaintance whom they felt might know the target person or at least someone who might know him or her. The person to whom the package was given was asked to act in the same manner until the package reached its destination.

Milgram sent 160 packages, of which 42 reached their destinations. The participants estimated that the limiting circumstance – handing over the package only to a personal acquaintance – would require at least one hundred mediators before it would reach its destination. All were surprised to learn that the average number of mediators was five to seven, very close indeed to Karinthy's original idea.

Thus was born the expression "six degrees of separation," which represents the theory that each human being on the face of the earth is connected to all other humans in a chain of acquaintances that is no more than six on average.

Playwright John Guare brought the expression to popular attention with his 1990 play of that name, followed by the film version in 1993. "I read somewhere that everybody on this planet is separated by only six other people," observes one of the characters in this sympathetic play based on a true story about an intelligent gay man who deceives New York society of the 1980s by posing as the son of Sidney Poitier. "Six degrees of separation between us and everyone else on this planet. The President of the United States, a gondolier in Venice, just fill in the names. I find that extremely comforting, that we're so close, but I also find it like Chinese water torture that we're so close because you have to find the right six people to make the connection. It's not just big names – it's anyone. A native in a rain forest, a Tiero del Fuegan, an Eskimo. I am bound – you are bound – to everyone on this planet by a trail of six people...everyone is a new door, opening into other worlds."

Now swap each of the characters the actress refers to with a potential business partner. The fact that only six handshakes separate you from him or her is one of the kingpins of globalization. From the time it was discovered, this concept has fired the imagination of many people, spawning everything from a mistaken genealogical theory of interconnected families to the campus favorite "Six Degrees of Separation from Kevin Bacon." As could be expected, it did not take long before the phenomenon would be studied by business theorists. Researchers from the Wharton School of Business investigated the connection between the number of degrees that separate any two members of the board of directors of a company and managerial salaries at that company. Indeed, in companies with board members separated by only a few degrees before joining the board, managerial salaries were higher.

In 2001 Duncan Watts and his colleagues at Columbia University set out to measure the influence of email in shrinking the world. Reenacting Milgram's historic experiment, 61,168 participants from 168 countries were asked to send emails to eighteen different addresses, including those of a Norwegian veterinarian, an Australian policeman and a Siberian university student.

Here, too, as in the original experiment, the participants were asked to make contact with the target by sending emails to personal acquaintances who they figured had a good chance of being connected to the target. And as if by magic – and like the original experiment – the average number of mediators was five to seven.

In West's opinion, email as a medium does not qualitatively change the manner in which we build social connections. In his experiments only 6% of all mediators were chosen uniquely by acquaintances via the internet; in fact, most mediators were connected to the senders through their shared place of employment. Interestingly, messages sent between two members of the same sex had a greater chance of reaching their target.

In this experiment, as with the original, the number of chains successfully completed – i.e., the emails that reached their targets – was relatively low. The intriguing question that arises from this is whether there is a common denominator between the people who are successful in delivering the message to its final destination.

Dr. Richard Wiseman, a professor of psychology at the University of Hertfordshire in England, has an interesting answer. Wiseman, an ex-professional magician and author of the book *The Luck Factor*, recently repeated the experiment in the U.K. The participants who were most successful in getting their packages to reach their targets were people who defined themselves as lucky in life. Those people, who stood out as well in their ability to cultivate a wide social circle, were particularly excited about making use of their connections for the experiment.

In other words, if you have a "package" to pass along, you may just find that your social network is quite a bit broader than you think, as long as you have the self-confidence necessary for making use of it. The world, for its part, is small enough.

◦◦

PART II:
DARWIN, INC.

Evolutionary psychology is the crossroads where cognitive psychology meets evolutionary biology. Its principles give us a clearer understanding of our place in the greater world. Moreover, evolutionary psychology shows us that a wide range of human behaviors is impelled by Darwin's theory of natural selection: a cautious approach to business, a loathing of insects, a reluctance to leave food on our plate, our social and sexual preferences.... You choose.

One of the most significant scientific developments in recent years has been the deciphering of the human genome. This project has taught us a great deal about our place in the animal kingdom. When we compared the human genome with the genome of our closest relative, the chimpanzee, we discovered that they are almost identical: they overlap by 98.76%. This comes as a blow to our preferred perception of man's dominance over other creatures. But even once we acknowledge our humble status, we are left with another equally challenging question: What is the role of the remaining 1.24% that distinguishes us from chimps? While it is true that our mastery of language enables us to write about chimpanzees – a uniquely human ability – this skill is not the primary difference. What really distinguishes humans from our evolutionary forefathers is our ability to travel mentally into the future. Man is the only creature in nature that can imagine future scenarios that aren't direct outcomes of the present. This unique gift is a relatively recent development – about three million years old, which in evolutionary terms is a blink of the eye. (Bear in mind that the first brain appeared on earth 500 million years ago.) In this relatively short time period, the human brain doubled in size, and the frontal lobe, which enables us to think about and plan for the future, became much more sophisticated.

We still don't understand exactly how this skill developed. We do know, however, that it allows us to trust and to experience joy. Because we can imagine the future, we are able to trust each other, hoping that at some future point in time, the other person will reciprocate. Our special ability also allows us to plan our lives, and to make decisions that will bring us closer to our goals. Much of our happiness, in fact, comes from our ability to imagine the future.

But being able to imagine different possibilities has another, very important, implication. The ability to envision the future has transformed man into the only creature aware of his inevitable death. All of mythology centers on the notion of man's struggle to guarantee himself immortality (that is, when it isn't showing us how the gods bicker with each other in a suspiciously mortal manner).

The cultural heritage of humanity – literature, art, music – would be impoverished were it not for the realization that we must leave a legacy before we are wiped off the face of the planet. Entrepreneurs, too, are driven by the need to leave a footprint in the sand of the business world. For most of them, economic success is secondary to their desire to make a mark; mostly, it functions as a tool to measure their achievements. And needless to say, this book, too, would never have been written had I been blessed with eternal life.

My exploration of evolutionary psychology also allowed me to acknowledge our modest place in our world. One of the proven ways to strengthen modesty and humility is to think of the world in cosmic terms. If we were to say, for the sake of argument, that the entire world was created in a single day, our species wouldn't have existed until the last two seconds. How much hubris could such an insignificant creature muster?

The main concepts that fill our waking days, and keep us from sleeping soundly at night, have been around for only a fraction of a second in evolutionary terms. The idea of "romantic love," as we know it today, is only six hundred years old. The theory of probability that is the basis of most business strategies is only three hundred years old. The materialism that drives today's consumer-centered economy is less than two hundred years old. And the concept of a "career," in its current form, began to develop only one hundred and fifty years ago.

Humility is the trait I value above all others, particularly in people who have succeeded in their careers. In a world in which success is everything, it takes tremendous spiritual strength to remain humble. Although I have made a lot of progress in my own attempt to overcome arrogance, I also know that I still have a long way to go. I can now admit that many of my best ideas, even in this book, are rooted in the ideas of others. I also realize that "humility is like underwear — necessary, but indecent if it shows." And for humility's sake, I will add that these words are not my own, but were written by the author Helen Nielsen.

Although man's predominance over chimpanzees is widely recognized, the fact is that when it comes to business, it is the genes that we share that matter the most.

Anyone who believes, as I do, that evolutionary psychology influences our behavior, will not be surprised to learn that the behavioral programming of our primitive brain overrides the newer parts of the brain responsible for cognitive decision-making. This is true in all realms, including the business world. In fact, evolutionary psychology is equipped with a toolkit that can explain what causes us to behave in a way that contradicts our best interests.

Evolution is built on two fundamental concepts that determine our behavior: survival and reproduction.

Survival is the evolutionary principle that causes our brains to be constantly on the lookout for potential threats. Our ancestors' ability to quickly identify danger often meant the difference between life and death. But the importance of survival, as it was imprinted on our brains eons ago, stands in the way of our ability to make solid investment choices. Mother Nature doesn't care about probability. The time it would have taken for one of our ancestors to calculate the likelihood of a potential threat could have cost him his life. From nature's point of view, we're better off worrying about 99 potential threats that never actually happen than not planning for the one threat that does materialize.

Above all, however, we are programmed to believe that if we perceive a threat where none exists, nature does not penalize us. Our mistake was for the greater good of survival. From an evolutionary standpoint, we are not equipped to face the challenge of identifying economic trends and potential economic threats, and we are programmed to define them before they have had a chance to crystallize. The primitive mindset that leads us to make these rash business decisions is designed to minimize risk, to safeguard our resources, and to give greater weight to negative events that pose a threat. Never mind that if we took the risk, we'd be likely to gain, or that the chances of a given threat are very slim. This part of our brains has no interest in probability, especially negative probability. Moreover, our primitive brains are not equipped to deal with situations that combine emotions and reason.

Because it is our emotional mind that keeps an eye out for potential hazards, its response time is twice that of the rational mind. When we buy and sell shares, for example, we are employing reason. Nature rewards us for early (and at times premature) identification of danger, and is more concerned with survival than with overreacting. In business, however, the opposite is true. The market penalizes us for acting impulsively. In a world that is drowning in information, it is not uncommon to falsely identify a trend, or to overreact because of a surplus of data.

The principle of survival also explains our unique ability to recognize betrayal. When our ancestors wandered through the African savanna hundreds of thousands of year ago, it was essential for them to sniff out any tribe member that was taking from the tribe without giving anything back. The ability to detect duplicity became a survival mechanism. At the same time, the ability to be duplicitous became equally useful.

The connection between the second rule of evolution (reproduction and its correlate, sexual activity) and happiness needs no elaboration. But in evolutionary terms, reproduction is defined as the availability of healthy and suitable mates. Evolution commands us to reproduce as much as possible, and to allow our genes – the carriers of our unique traits – to be transmitted to as many offspring as possible. Our success in this mission is a direct translation of natural selection, the evolutionary process that favors survivors. People who scatter their genes through the population are considered successful.

We can interpret the pursuit of status that is so prevalent in our society as an attempt to increase the pool of potential mates. In this respect, too, we are not that different from chimpanzees, which are prepared to attack (and even to kill) anyone who threatens their status.

I am convinced that evolutionary psychology can explain many of our decisions, especially the wrong ones. In addition, I believe that the importance of this nascent field of research goes beyond this. If the principal theme of this book is the freedom of choice that remains in our hands, evolutionary psychology represents the lack of free choice. When we make a decision, we may think we are choosing freely, but the fact is that our forebears are making the choice for us.

෨෧

CAUTION: NATURAL SELECTION IN ACTION

ᘒ

*"Man with all his noble qualities, with sympathy which feels
for the most debased, with benevolence which extends not only to
other men but to the humblest living creature, with his god-like
intellect which has penetrated into the movements and constitu-
tion of the solar system - with all these exalted powers, Man still
bears in his bodily frame the indelible stamp of his lowly origin."*
— Charles Darwin, *The Descent of Man*

Investment Accident Waiting to Happen

Look up to the sky and gaze at the clouds. What do you see there? "As you like it," Shakespeare might tell you in the third act of Hamlet. The following is a conversation between Hamlet and Lord Polonius, Ophelia's father:

> HAMLET: Do you see yonder cloud that's almost in shape of a camel?
> LORD POLONIUS: By the mass, and 'tis like a camel, indeed.
> HAMLET: Methinks it is like a weasel.
> LORD POLONIUS: It is backed like a weasel.
> HAMLET: Or like a whale?
> LORD POLONIUS: Very like a whale.

Shakespeare is well acquainted with the human tendency to search out patterns and shapes that hold significance in the world around us. In fact, the source of this skill in recognizing patterns is rooted in an ancient and essential need. Natural selection rewards capabilities that improve chances for survival. The ability to recognize patterns that represent a threat – such as beasts of prey – and subsequently taking the required action became an important tool in the struggle for existence waged by early man, a matter of life and death. At the same time, nature did not demand a price for incorrectly identifying a pattern; in terms of survival, this meant that many false alarms were preferable to a single failure to recognize a real danger.

Thus, the human brain developed the ability, based on pattern recognition, to come to conclusions and decide in an instant. Nature rewards survivors with the chance to sire children blessed with the same genetic baggage, including this ability. This is Darwin at his best. In the principles of natural selection, Darwin obeys that most sweeping rule of them all: the law of entropy. According to this law, it is easier for a certain system to break down than to maintain its structure. That is the reason for the pressure that natural selection exerts so that important knowledge will be encoded genetically, thus bringing down the high cost of human learning.

This knowledge often takes the form of what we tend to call intuitive, or heuristic, behavior. Intuitive behavior places a heavy emphasis on the connection between the brain and the eye. The French philosopher René Descartes claimed that "…it is the soul that sees, not the eye." The ease with which the brain leads the eye astray has no better expression than the dialogue from Hamlet quoted above.

Studies show that during the stage in which the brain incorporates the pattern it has imbued with some sort of meaning, it is more likely to tend toward negative, rather than positive, interpretation of the pattern. Researchers see this, too, as a return to ancient human behavior that warns against ignoring negative scenarios, which may exact a heavy price.

Indeed, if you follow your thoughts in a stream of consciousness you will find that they generally stop and dwell on the negative. Those thoughts are better at grabbing and holding on to our attention than positive or neutral thoughts. That is the way our creator fashioned us in order to protect us from possible threats.

The problem begins when the world around us presents us with a vast array of patterns – shapes and numbers, for example, most of which contain no meaning other than coincidence. The philosopher and mathematician Frank Ramsey dedicated his short life (he died in 1930 at the age of 28) to the study of chaos. He claimed that every instance of alleged disorder is in fact a matter of scale, that it is possible to find every mathematical object if one searched a big enough universe for it. Carl Sagan – astronomer, author, and host of the television show "Cosmos" – said that in many cases people raise their eyes skyward and see, for example, eight stars that form a nearly straight line, tempting them to believe that these stars were placed in a row like some galactic lighthouse leading the way. In fact, Sagan said, if you look at a large enough group of stars you can see almost anything you want, as with astrological signs. That is Ramsey's theory in action.

A simple example can be found in Ramsey's Series, which is often used in mathematics competitions. If the first 101 whole numbers are arranged in any order it will always be possible to find eleven numbers in a row that form a rising or descending series (thought not necessarily contiguous numbers). In other words, the possibility of finding a pattern depends largely on the size and scope of the field being observed.

So, what do we have here? On the one hand, an intelligent creature equipped genetically with the need and ability to recognize patterns. On the other hand, an infinite statistical field that creates endless patterns, most of which are completely meaningless. If this intelligent creature also invests money in the stock market and bases its decisions on recognizing patterns in the market, then it is headed for an unavoidable investment accident. An investment accident in this case is the decision to buy or sell a stock earlier than is fitting due to having recognized a pattern that does not in fact exist. Since the brain tends toward negative scenarios, the cognitive errors will be on the side of pessimism and cynicism, resulting in a sale.

Let's say that you have decided, on principle, that you will sell a stock after five successive days of falling prices. The statistical probability that you will hit this particular pattern is fairly high − nearly once in six weeks. If you sell, you are most likely doing so for the wrong reason, since the pattern you recognized was random. Nature may not punish people for mistakenly recognizing patterns, but financial loss in the stock market is a common punishment.

The chance of having an investment accident is the meeting point between two worlds: our genetic makeup, which searches for patterns, and statistics, the major provider of random patterns. The point at which they converge is familiar to anyone who has ever invested in the stock market, and it is called "overconfidence." Overconfidence is the trait that causes 80% of us (according to research) to think that we are better drivers than the average, that we will live a longer life span than the average, and that we have a better sense of humor than the average. It is also what causes 70% of lawyers to believe that their case is stronger than their opponent's. Incidentally, overconfidence is particularly prevalent in conditions where information is plentiful and feedback is minimal – the ultimate fertilizer.

Overconfidence is not irrational behavior in the world of finance. It creates credibility. Making full use of information (even if it is incorrect), confidence, assertiveness – all these hold a high social value. But as a result of overconfidence we exaggerate our powers of prognostication and tend to recognize patterns in completely random data, or make wrong assumptions about the underlying factors of chance events. Unfortunately, aptitude in advanced statistics, which would prevent investment accidents of this sort, does not tend to come hand in hand with well honed social skills.

The erroneous recognition of patterns is not in and of itself a problem; the conclusions drawn and the decisions to act, are. Overconfidence is precisely the detonator that turns decision into action and sparks an investment accident.

Of all the overconfidence bestowed on the world, men took more than their fair share. Women, with less, are therefore better investors when faced with similar circumstances to those of men.

So, how can investment accidents be avoided? Self awareness as to overconfidence and humble behavior are two steps in the right direction. CNN founder Ted Turner apparently missed that lesson. He once said, "If I only had a little humility, I'd be perfect."

ᘐᘐ

Firstborn Children Are Not Gamblers

As an only child I have often wondered how my life would be different had I had a brother or a sister or even a few of them as a child. That question arose again and took on new meaning when Professor Carlo Strenger of Tel Aviv University and I undertook a study of entrepreneurship. The challenge was to try to discover whether it was possible to identify a common denominator among the personality traits of successful entrepreneurs. Birth order was one of the variables we investigated in our interviews, but the small sample of entrepreneurs used in the study made it hard to reach any clear-cut conclusions about the connection between birth order and that intriguing question, "Are entrepreneurs born or made?"

Those who believe in the former have scientific findings, made available in recent years, to prove them right. One of these was mentioned in Dr. Peter J. D'Adamo's book *Eat Right 4 Your Type*, in which he claims that self-made people in the United States are four times more likely to have B-type blood than what is expected in the general population. But even people who believe that an entrepreneurial spirit is something you are born with cannot ignore the fact that the jobs of US president and UK prime minister have been filled in striking numbers by firstborn sons and that the revolutionary theories in science, culture and the arts are more likely to be introduced by the middle child or the youngest sibling.

With regards to entrepreneurship, the connection to birth order is particularly elusive and has not been subjected to extensive research. That notwithstanding, the hundreds of interviews I have conducted have left me with the feeling that it indeed exists, although it is quite complex. In general, it seems to me that firstborn children are more suited to managerial roles, while their younger siblings will be relatively more successful as entrepreneurs. This is based on experience, but of course there are exceptions, some of which have cost me business opportunities that I failed to take.

And what does science have to say about it? As usual, it depends on who you ask: the sociologist, the psychologist, or the evolutionary psychologist, whose work is grounded in Darwin's theory of evolution.

The sociologist's point of view is represented by Dalton Conley in his book *The Pecking Order*, which is based on data collected by the United States Census and interviews with families. Conley makes the claim that middle children have a lower chance of receiving the financial backing they need to pursue their education; their chances of studying in a private school drop by 25% with the arrival of a younger sibling and their chance of repeating a grade rises several times. Birth order therefore takes on significance not as a psychological factor but as a drain on family financial resources. What is new in Conley's book is the claim that family is the source of inequality and not, as was generally accepted, the refuge from inequality. The missing link for our purposes is the connection between private education and entrepreneurship, which has never been proved. What is more, most entrepreneurs I have interviewed do not have an MBA, and if they do, it is rarely from a prestigious business school.

The family as resource is exactly the point of departure for Frank Sulloway's brilliant and unique book *Born to Rebel* (1992). However, Sulloway defines the family resources in the evolutionary terms used earlier, such as parental attention, the limited resource over which children fight. Sulloway claims that firstborn children naturally identify with power and authority. As the first to reach the family framework they make use of their size and power to retain their special status. Firstborns are more assertive and dominant than their younger siblings, more ambitious, more fanatical about their status, more conservative and self-assured. Their younger siblings, on the other hand, start from a position of inferiority and so question and challenge the status quo, developing rebellious personalities. As scientists, for example, they are the ones to come out against existing scientific theories and will present or support new ones. But how? What in the family dynamic brings this about?

According to Darwinists, personality is the sum total of the strategies a person adopts in his or her youth to survive, and, later in life, to reproduce. Sibling rivalry, they claim, is ultimately all about surviving childhood successfully.

In the competition for the limited resource of parental attention, siblings take on strategies that are affected mainly by their sex, by their differences in age and by their birth order. Later in life, say the Darwinists, they continue to apply these strategies in the business world as well.

"Sometimes a child who has lost his power, the small kingdom he ruled, understands better than others the importance of power and authority." That is how Alfred Adler, a second son and disciple of Freud who rebelled against him, defined the feelings of a firstborn son presented with a brother or sister.

In this evolutionary context, firstborn sons are the alpha males of primate society, the super apes. Their strategy is clear and focused on domination. They are the future CEOs and politicians. Their younger brothers, as with primates of a lower status, work hard from childhood to improve their social qualifications and cooperative skills. Domination and cooperation are the two basic strategies that have been created and reproduced in hundreds of ways of Darwinist selection; neither is necessarily preferable to the other and both can lead to success.

Still, a propensity toward sociability and cooperation is only one of the strategies that non-firstborns adopt. In their battle for parental attention, they must create for themselves a special niche that is all their own. The main strategy available to them is that of divergence, the natural strategy for younger siblings, since it creates new realms that are outside the natural territory of firstborns, thus reducing the competition. This strategy is likely to win the desired parental support, and in any event help the younger siblings become less dependent on them. Indeed, non-firstborns are characterized by curiosity and openness to experimentation – in our case, as a part of the process of forming a strategy that can distinguish them from their older siblings – making them willing to take risks. These are the rebels, the innovators, and also the social collaborators. Are they also future entrepreneurs?

Frank Sulloway did not deal with this entrepreneurial aspect, but his research enables extrapolation. He painstakingly compiled a database of the resumes of 3,890 scientists and researchers from the eighteenth and nineteenth centuries. His main interests were how these people related to new theories, what their travel habits were (many researched nature) and other characteristics. But first and foremost, Sulloway classified his subjects according to birth order. His impressive database included eighty-three pairs of siblings. This unusual sample enabled the investigation of such factors as openness to innovation among members of the same family.

Analysis of the data provides exceptional results by any scientific standard. The chance that a non-firstborn will support a new theory is 7.3 times greater than a firstborn from the same family. Such an interesting insight is likely to explain the overwhelming opposition of French scientists in the nineteenth century to Darwin's theory of evolution and other new theories, claims Sulloway. In 1859, the year in which *On the Origin of Species* was published, French families averaged only 1.1 children per family, as opposed to 2.8 in other countries. In other words, the vast majority of French researchers would have been only children, or firstborns, and therefore conservative. Thus, fables of national character are born.

Sulloway's wide-ranging study also dealt with the issue of the connection between readiness to assume risk and birth order. It is important to note that from a Darwinist point of view, the evolutionary price of risk-taking is very reasonable in a situation of little chance for survival and reproduction. Thus, risk-taking is a useful strategy for occupying a special niche and, consequently, for gaining parental attention.

Against the backdrop of the clear limitations in getting these nineteenth-century scientists to speak up, Sulloway chose to exchange the element of risk for a representative element that could be measured: the willingness of these researchers to engage in journeys for their research. After all, expeditions in the nineteenth century were often fraught with danger. Charles Darwin's famed ship the Beagle lost no fewer than five crew members during its voyage of 1831 to 1836, and Darwin himself was seriously ill more than once during the expedition. To put it bluntly, at that time, journeys to far flung corners of the globe represented an efficient way of shortening one's life expectancy.

The findings of Sulloway's research were once again clear and unequivocal. Non-firstborns were twice as likely to risk their lives on expeditions as firstborns. Youngest children were even more likely, fully three times more so than firstborns. Darwin himself, the fifth of six children, agreed to sail with the Beagle when his teacher, John Stevens Henslow, turned down the offer. Henslow was, as could be expected, a firstborn son.

So much for the Darwinists. But will a psychologist's approach add another dimension to the debate? A good place to start is with the research of Dr. Kevin Leman, an American authority on parenting who has published a number of books on the topic. According to Leman, firstborn children tend toward conservatism, punctiliousness and perfectionism. Middle children, sandwiched in between siblings, tend to look for appreciation outside the family framework, and the youngest siblings possess the most highly developed social skills. Dr. Leman claims that only children have the characteristics of firstborns.

In 1977, Dr. Leman conducted a study relevant to the topic at hand, albeit on a small number of participants (31). According to the U.S. Census Bureau, the chance of being a firstborn or only child is 49.2%; the chance of being a youngest sibling is 32.8%; and the chance of being a middle child is 18%. Dr. Leman discovered that of all self-employed people, more than 50%, or three times their number in the population, were likely to be middle children, while only 40% – half their representation in the general population – were firstborns and youngest siblings.

Firstborns, Dr. Leman claims, feel most comfortable within the status quo, and they work best within an organizational framework. In contrast, middle children tend to break away from their families and identify with outside elements. In business terms, this means that they find satisfaction outside the organization.

An additional finding of interest refers to the youngest siblings. While other siblings are engaged in a variety of occupations, youngest siblings overwhelmingly (80%) tend to be involved in service professions. Youngest siblings are known for their interpersonal skills, which of course are at the foundation of the service industry.

In another, unofficial, survey, Dr. Leman investigated the connection between membership in a CEO club and birth order. From among 224 members, only four were middle children. Nearly all the others were firstborn or only children.

So why aren't firstborn children gamblers? One of the psychological theories I have come across – albeit, a far-fetched one – claims that most heavy gamblers are not firstborn or only children, but younger siblings who lost in the battle for parental attention. Now, as gamblers, they can console themselves with the thought that they are losing because luck has betrayed them and not because they are inferior to their older siblings.

And if we are talking about making a wager, and your office uses a one-line résumé, then when your company is looking for a CEO make sure to note the birth order of your candidates. A firstborn CEO is your best bet. But if it's an entrepreneur you want, you may have better luck with a non-firstborn child.

Does Trust Pay?

If you ask people in the business world, most will say that trust is a central and critical element in doing business, especially in their own successful career. Economists have been saying for years that trust is the lubricant necessary for business and the main component of social capital. In the age of global economics, trusting others is a prerequisite for doing business.

However, scouring various resources for the term "trust" paints a much darker picture of human nature. Six of every seven quotes on the subject warn the reader of the consequences of trusting others, of which American humorist Peter Dunne Finley's statement that you should "trust everybody, but cut the cards" is only one example.

The attempt at settling the difference between human nature and the need for trust in business dealings leads the inquisitive scholar to biologists specializing in evolution. Richard Dawkins, author of *The Selfish Gene*, one of the most prominent practitioners in the field, actually does partially manage to bridge the gap between the two approaches. Dawkins claims that humans, without doubt the crowning glory of creation, are still a part of the evolutionary process and motivated by their most basic genetic impulses: survival and reproduction. In life's complex circumstances, placing one's trust in another – and even more so, altruistic behavior – threatens survival, and thus, the ability to reproduce. Or, in Dawkins' words, "If you want to build a society in which individuals cooperate unselfishly, you can expect little help from biological nature."

However, humans are different from all other creations in their capacity for conscious foresight. A person can envision a future scenario that is a possible outcome of a certain action or failure. This ability enables him to sacrifice a short-term interest in favor of the highly beneficial actualization of a long-term interest. In other words, the human imagination allows people to rise up against their own creator and choose an option that involves an element of trust and even concessions rather than short-term benefit, by assuming that the risk will pay off in the future.

How is the level of interpersonal trust measured for each individual? Most research conducted in this field in recent years has posed one simple question to those being studied: Please place yourself in one of the two following categories – those who believe that, generally speaking, most people can be trusted, or those who believe that you can't be too careful when dealing with others. This simple classification has proved itself in hundreds of studies carried out in the past twenty years.

The considerable research done on this topic can be divided in two: that which relates to the national and cultural level and that which relates to the personal.

Trust on a National Level
A study conducted in May 2005 by The Guardian among its readers set out to investigate the moral values of British citizens. The question used to assess this issue was: "A break-in has occurred in the home of your closest friends.

In your opinion, will they report the true value of their household goods, or will they exaggerate their insurance claims?"

It was readily apparent that "your closest friends" actually meant those being surveyed themselves. By referring to good friends – who would most naturally be of a similar socio-demographic background and a similar value system – the researcher stands a better chance of receiving a true and honest answer since the survey participant will not feel the risk of personal ramifications inherent in such an answer.

The good news is that half of all Britons would not inflate their claims as a matter of principle. The bad news is that two-thirds of those in the age group 18 to 24 would, in fact, inflate their demands and are therefore not trustworthy. Trust is restored for those over 65; 3/4 of this group would not exaggerate their claims. However, would the answer to the question posed by The Guardian have been different if posed in another country with a different cultural makeup, or even in England during a different period? Absolutely – and the differences are stunning: The level of trust that Norwegians gave their friends in 1995 is twenty times greater than that of Brazil (see chart).

Trust, Income, Culture & Religion

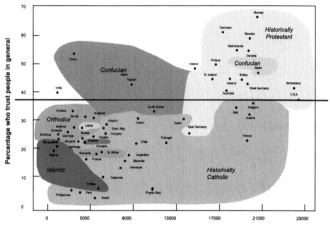

GNP / capita (World Bank purchasing power partly estimates, 1995 U.S.

Source: Inglehart 1999

To economists' delight, it really pays off. On the national level, most researchers agree, a trusting attitude has a positive effect on income – the correlation between the level of interpersonal trust that characterizes a country and its economic welfare, as measured by per capita GNP, is high, more than 0.6. The US serves as a watershed here; an interpersonal trust level of 0.35 means that 35% of Americans believe that most people are trustworthy. If that sounds low, think about this: the United States enjoyed an interpersonal trust level of 60% only forty years ago.

So how is it that the trust level has plunged to nearly half its original level? Apparently, that is the unavoidable role of the American media, especially television, in the past few decades. The high level of exposure to decision-makers and the well-oiled machinery of criticism and scrutiny that faces them do not inspire trust. In fact, there is one country on this curve that provides an exception: economic welfare in China is severely limited but the level of interpersonal trust is quite high. Thus, China's position on the curve strengthens the opinion of those who believe in its untapped potential; if the economists researching trust are right, China will move toward its rightful place in the curve as dictated by the correlation between the level of trust and economic welfare of a country.

The true drama concealed in these data is that most countries have only a limited ability to change their position on the chart in any meaningful manner. The reason is embedded in two types of feedback that cannot be reconciled. Citizens of countries characterized by a high level of trust enjoy positive feedback of a virtuous circle, which generally results in pay off for risk-taking, so that their assets increase and their belief in trust is reinforced. Citizens of the poorer countries, on the other hand, are faced with high risk of a vicious circle. Since level of trust, according to the study, is low in those countries, trusting others could prove quite costly since the trusting person has few assets to lose at the outset. These two types of feedback cycles exist side by side and provide an additional explanation to the issue found at the top of the worldwide agenda – the gap between developed and developing nations. It is therefore no surprise that Edward S. Banfield, who researched the immense economic discrepancy between southern and northern Italy, discovered, in his pioneering research in the late 1950s, that the differing levels of interpersonal trust between the two parts of Italy was huge.

Interpersonal trust is a cultural value that was embedded in societies long before the Industrial Revolution or the important economic developments of the previous centuries. It is therefore interesting to explore the discrepancy in trust issues between countries on the basis of other cultural characteristics, such as religion. The chart on page 130 reveals that there is a strong connection between the level of trust and religious faith. Thirteen of the eighteen countries found on the top of the list for interpersonal trust are largely Protestant; three are Confucian, one Hindi and only one Catholic (Ireland). Of the thirteen countries on the lower half of the list, fully eight are Catholic.

How can this wide discrepancy between different Christian denominations be explained? Most likely in the nature of control exercised in the different religious institutions. While the Catholic Church is very centralized and bureaucratic, Protestant believers enjoy a more community-based structure in which they maintain a certain level of control, and this geographic proximity encourages trust. It is no surprise that the Protestant countries ranking low on the trust scale are those that were part of the Communist bloc – which was centralized, bureaucratic and arbitrary.

So, does trust pay? Absolutely. Trustworthiness, on the other hand, does not pay in every situation. Trustworthiness, we are told by Edward L. Glaeser of the Department of Economics at Harvard, does not pay in countries where the level of interpersonal trust is low. It does, however, pay in countries with a high level of interpersonal trust. This is little comfort.

Trust, according to the research, fosters trustworthiness, which means that in countries with a high level of trust there are more citizens – and businesspeople – who are trustworthy, so then the cycle of positive feedback can take care of the rest. On a national level, trusting others pays off financially and this cultural, ethical characteristic of interpersonal trust is reinforced to become part of the foundation of the society. On the personal level – the other category studied – the story is altogether different.

Trust on a Personal Level

Try to recall the last business deal you were involved in. More precisely, the signing of the contract. Handshakes were exchanged, wineglasses clinked, and if the deal was big enough, one of the signatories left the room to chat with journalists. At that point in time, the two celebrating signatories had become familiar with one another to a point, their lawyers and accountants had left no stone unturned, part of the financial considerations was supposed to depend on financial milestones, and if the worst case scenario happened and one of the sides did not fulfill its obligations, the injured party could still go to court to try to have the deal enforced or be compensated.

This deal is typical of many deals in the business world. It is significantly different than the one-time deals we make on a daily basis, from riding in a taxi to ordering a moving van to selling property. In contrast to the deal described, with day-to-day deals the element of prior reputation is relatively limited or even nonexistent, long-term strategy is irrelevant and there is practically no mechanism for correcting mistakes. This is the source of the higher risk involved, both in economic terms and especially in emotional terms.

The ability to bridge the gap between the popular belief that one should not trust one's fellow man and the attitude of businesspeople – that trust is a central element in business without which it is very difficult to succeed –is a reflection of the ability to distinguish between two types of deals: the one-time deal and the relationship-building deal.

That is precisely the reason that behavioral scientists are interested in one-time deals. Their focus is the element of emotional risk experienced by someone who chooses to trust others by placing his fate in their hands. Popular faith may claim that one should not trust others but studies provide surprising evidence for circumstances in which trust does pay.

While economists plan their experiments under the assumption that human behavior is rational and geared toward maximizing gains, people in the behavioral sciences know that man's nature is far more complex; a risk aversion, a subjective perception of the concept of a "fair deal," and a feeling of being discriminated against are just a few of the human biases liable to stand between a person and rational economic behavior in economists' terms.

Most of the research in this field is based on relatively simple games that enable players who do not know one another to be tracked in different situations involving trust. These games also serve to assess the effect of sociodemographic traits on their preferences.

In order to demonstrate the first game, imagine for a moment that you are on a Caribbean cruise. You have disembarked on the beach of one of the area's pleasant islands and the shadow that falls across your footsteps turns out to be a local photographer who makes his living from taking pictures of tourists. Come evening, when you return to the ship laden with impressions, you are not totally surprised at the sight of the photograph lying on a makeshift table next to the ship's gangplank. Your face smiling in the Caribbean sun adorns this particularly excellent photo. "How much?" you ask. "Ten," answers the photographer.

Hundreds of passengers make their way up the gangplank. There is little time before the ship sails. If you wish to buy the photograph, now is the time. You and the photographer are both aware of the particular balance of power in the negotiations between you. You are about to leave this place, apparently forever, and the price you offer for the photographs is a now or never proposal. If the photographer accepts your offer you will pay that price and the photograph will be yours. If you offer too little money, you run the risk that the photographer will be unwilling to part with it (though it is clear he has no use for it), since he thinks your offer is unfair or perhaps insults his professional prestige or will have an effect on the other passengers waiting to embark. So how much will you offer for this one-time souvenir in the few seconds remaining to you, a one-time offer with no chance for negotiations? The moment you have named your price, the result of the process no longer depends on you.

The Ultimatum Game

The situation in the Caribbean, examples of which you will find in your daily life as well, was chosen by behavioral science researchers as a focus for one of the most diverse studies on the subject of trust and turned into a lab rat game called the Ultimatum Game.

The game works like this: two anonymous players flip a coin. The winner receives, say, one hundred dollars. He decides how much to offer the one who was less lucky than he. The second player can either accept or reject this proposal. If the second player accepts, the money is split according to the proposal and if the second player rejects, neither player receives anything. Both players are aware of the rules of the game.

How would you act if you were the winner? If you listen to the economists you will try to maximize your gains by offering as little as possible to the loser. Economists believe in rational behavior; in their opinion, the loser should be willing to make do with whatever he is offered. In fact, this strategy only works in primitive societies (Papua New Guinea; Mongolia; the rainforests, etc.) according to one study, and between very young children in another. In the vast majority of the other cases studied, this approach left both players empty-handed.

So, how much would you offer to the loser if you won? It quickly becomes apparent that your answer depends on your sex, cultural background, educational level, testosterone level and a host of other variables, but most especially, the level of trust that characterizes you.

Most of the people tested in the lab experiment offered 40-50% of the sum won. Half of the losers spurned offers of less than 20%.

The Dictator Game
Suppose for a moment that you decided to allocate your winnings fifty-fifty with the loser of the game. This is clearly a matter of generosity. What part of that decision comes from altruism and what part from an approach inspired by a strategy, i.e., from an expectation of reciprocity from the

other? Or, in what measure does the decision to pass along fifty dollars come from the fear that a lower offer will be rejected so that your portion will be forfeited?

One of the ways of answering this question – at least in the lab – is by presenting a second game, the very simplest in this context. It is called the Dictator Game and these are the rules: two players flip a coin and the winner is asked how much (if any) of the winnings he wishes to share with the loser. The loser accepts whatever the winner gives (or does not give) him. End of game.

Clearly, there is no room for strategizing in this game, since the "proposer" is in no way dependent on the "responder's" answer. If the proposer does indeed offer a sum at all, this is an expression of altruism, albeit not entirely purely so, since in lab conditions the proposer may wish to make an impression on the researcher whereas in real life, perhaps, this could be his life partner. Most proposers offer 10-20% of their winnings in this game: 20% under usual conditions and 10% when the offer is made anonymously. A researcher who guaranteed an extensive system for ensuring the absolute anonymity of the players found that nearly half of the envelopes that were supposed to contain a certain sum were in fact empty.

It only takes a simple calculation to know what kind of effect is attributable to the strategic element in the Ultimatum Game and how much to altruism. If a combination of strategic and altruistic considerations causes a person to offer 40-50% of his winnings and if altruism alone yields 10-20%, one finds that strategy is responsible for two-thirds of the decision taken and altruism for one third, or less than that if participants are given full anonymity (to the joy of the evolutionists, whose faith in human goodness is naturally limited).

The Trust Game

So, does trust pay? To answer that question another game was devised – what else but the Trust Game? In this game as in the others, two players who do not know one another play one time only. The winner of the coin toss (player #1) receives one hundred dollars and he must decide how much – if anything – he will give to the other player (#2). The organizer of the game promises that he will triple whatever sum #1 gives to #2. Player #2 must then decide how much – if anything – he will give back to #1. The game ends there. Both players understand all the rules before playing.

Let's say that you are player #1 and you have just won one hundred dollars. How much will you offer player #2? If you give him fifty dollars it will be tripled to $150 and if he decides to share it with you equally then you will end up with $125, an improvement for both from the start of the game. If you hand over $33 then player #2 will receive $99, and if he gives you $30 only (and indeed 30% is the average sum returned in this game) then the trust you placed in him did not pay off. If you gave him the full $100 – a sign of absolute trust – then you have raised the pie to be shared to $300, which is the highest sum possible. If player #2 pays you half of it back for trusting him (thus proving himself also trustworthy) then you will share a total of $150 each.

Indeed, 25% of players #1 choose to express complete trust and hand over the entire sum to player #2. The risk is palpable – in the lab, 9% of the participants who received the money did not give back a cent – but retroactively it pays off since trustworthiness is not a fixed attribute; it depends on the level of trust someone places in you. The higher the level of trust, the more one is encouraged to be trustworthy. The big revelation here is that trustworthiness does increase with trust.

The scientific conclusions of this important study can be summed up as follows:

-   Trust in the Trust Game (as expressed through returning part of the sum of money won) pays off only marginally, if at all.
-   Trust very clearly pays off only if given completely, since trust promotes trustworthiness.

Of all these games, the Ultimatum Game is the most commonly used in lab experiments. Hundreds of studies have used this game to test the effect of various factors, including socio-demographic variables, on its results. The following summarizes some interesting findings:

Amount of Winnings

Many people feel that the amount of winnings has an effect on the behavior of players in the Ultimatum Game. Thus, for example, they estimate that when the amount is high, say $100,000 instead of the original $100, the winner will offer less than the 40-50% that players offer on the average. But there is no evidence of this in the research. The sum offered in these cases is indeed relatively lower, but not by that much. The explanation is simple: The winning player (#1) risks a significant amount. If he is primarily motivated by strategic considerations, he fears that a low offer will harm his chances of winning.

Sex

Unsurprisingly, both sexes expect to receive more from women but they offer more to men – about 15% in fact – which brings to light a lamentable and well-known social reality.

Still, and perhaps unexpectedly, men tend to be more trusting than women, while women are more trustworthy than men. This finding can be explained by the vulnerability of women in society. Women are more exposed to betrayals of trust, and the consequence is liable to take a higher emotional toll on them. A similar finding characterizes minority groups, which are also more vulnerable to betrayals of trust.

Furthermore, while men do not tend to offer more to women whom the researchers define as attractive, women offer 10% more to attractive men.

Age

In keeping with the expectations of economists, children behave more egotistically than adults. They offer as little as possible in order to maximize their gains and they are content with less when they are on the losing side. Children who are relatively tall for their age and sex surprisingly offer less in different games. Indeed, the height bonus is a well-known phenomenon in Western society. In the U.S., each additional inch of height is worth $750 in the annual wage a laborer earns.

Biology

The male hormone testosterone, which is found in higher amounts in football players and firemen, is low in priests and doctors and average in university professors and the unemployed.

In an interesting experiment using the Ultimatum Game among those testing for a high testosterone level, it turns out that men in this group offer more than expected but are quick to take offense when they are not offered what they consider to be enough. In this sense, testosterone can indeed be classified as a macho hormone.

The Truth About Lying

Mankind has been distorting the truth from its very first appearances in the Bible. Eve: "The serpent beguiled me, and I did eat." Cain: "Am I my brother's keeper?" And we've only gotten worse. Ask Psychologist Robert Feldman of the University of Massachusetts. According to his research, 60% of us lie at least once (and usually more than that) during every ten minutes of conversation.

It is just so easy to lie, Feldman tells us. We teach our children that honesty is the best policy but at the same time we expect them to pretend they like the birthday present they got from Aunt Sally. And then when they grow up we're on the receiving end of their sour grapes over this two-sided message we have been feeding them.

In another study, Jeff Hancock of Cornell University got thirty students to keep a personal communications journal for a period of two weeks, then afterward had them own up to the lies, half-truths and infelicities recorded in the journals. Hancock found that 14% of the emails contained lies, as did 21% of the text messages and 27% of the face-to-face conversations. Phone conversations told a particularly sad story: fully 37% sported at least one lie.

While people tend to lie less in media where there is documentation (like email), telephone conversations often involve situations in which unexpected questions demand immediate answers, like "How was your date last night?"

There are many reasons for lying. Fear of punishment (loss) is the reason shared by the heroes of the Bible and children. As we get older, our aspirations – for money, power, social standing – become the reasons for lying. Many of the lies we tell are there to cover up other lies we have told previously. But of course, there are serious limitations to the study of liars; after all, they can't be relied on to give the most truthful answers to researchers.

Another useful insight from Feldman's research has to do with the difference between the type of lies told by men as opposed to women. While there is no real difference in the amount of lying each does, one study shows that women lie in order to make their co-conversationalists feel better while men lie in order to make themselves feel better. Another concludes that women have developed better skills at detecting lies, and, according to Dory Hollander in *101 Lies Men Tell Women*, the most common lie men tell women is "I'll call you."

Lies are a daily part of the social fabric of our lives. While some of them harm friendships and trust between people, others play an important role in avoiding embarrassing situations and preserving vulnerable egos. It seems safe to say that our social lives would crumble under the burden of unrelenting truth.

In fact, according to a study done by Bella de Paulo, a psychologist at the University of Virginia, we tell ten to twenty times more lies in which we pretend to like something ("This cake is wonderful!") than we pretend not to like something ("I'll never vote for that two-faced snake of a guy").

If our unavoidable demise provides a central meaning to our lives, then one of the most significant elements in our long journey from birth to death is the constant tension that accompanies us in our attempts at revealing the lies and deceptions that surround us. Fairy tales like Pinocchio and Little Red Riding Hood enjoy tremendous popularity as folkloric reflections of this deep-seated truth. You would be hard-pressed to find a play by Shakespeare, that keen observer of humankind, that does not include at least one example.

An Israeli secret service agent whose expertise is in ferreting out lies once explained to me that the human brain actually prefers truth to lies. His method for detecting lies is based on content analysis and focuses on the uniqueness of the expressions used by a person who is failing to tell the truth. This expert claims that liars add all sorts of superfluous details to their stories, rarely tell their lies in the first person and employ almost no vocabulary that expresses emotion. Surprisingly, other words are missing too, words of discernment like "but" and "without." It appears that the human brain rids itself of its discomfort with lies by piling up some words and filtering out others. The only liars who hold up under interrogation are those who are unaware of their own lies, or, put differently, who lie first and foremost to themselves.

In his brilliant book *Why We Lie: The Evolutionary Roots of Deception*, evolutionary psychologist David Livingston Smith manages to seat Freud, Darwin and Machiavelli together at the poker table of life so that he can present an evolutionary explanation for the very same phenomenon described by the Israeli secret service agent.

Smith claims that the constant possibility of deception is a central element in the existence of plants and animals and especially humans. This possibility has an effect on all our relationships, including the most important of all – with ourselves. According to Smith, the ability to lie is a basic evolutionary necessity, like the ability to spot a lie in others. Early man developed a special ability to pick up on which of his hunter-gatherer friends was taking advantage of the group's limited resources and thus, with time, turned into a walking lie-detector.

The easiest way – evolutionarily speaking – for man to deceive his peers is to deceive himself first of all. By hiding the truth from ourselves we find it easier to hide it from others. Smith claims that the crucial event in human history that honed this skill was the appearance of language. From that point onward, the human brain developed a subconscious apparatus for ignoring various information and reality checks, keeping them even from ourselves. That is how man could continue to carry out deceptions without giving himself away, unlike those who knowingly lie.

In a rather surprising twist, it turns out that people who suffer from depression tend to lie less (to others or to themselves) than those who do not. Depressives have a better grasp on reality and a realistic understanding of the level of control they exert (or fail to exert) over different situations in their lives and the lives of others. This ability to discern led researcher Shelly Taylor of UCLA to determine that a certain level of self-deception is essential for our mental wellbeing. Anyone who has ever seen Arthur Miller's play *Death of a Salesman* surely recalls

Willy Loman's tragic fate when he can no longer continue deceiving himself.

There are clear evolutionary advantages to deception and self-deception. The most common self-deception is overestimation of our own abilities. Research shows that we believe ourselves to be better drivers, believe that we get along better with others, believe that we will live longer than our neighbors, believe that we are better investors than our peers, and of course that we are superior lovers. This phenomenon has positive repercussions on our ability to deal with daily setbacks effectively and plays a key role in one of the two essential evolutionary tests – survival.

The other evolutionary test – reproduction – apparently has nothing to do with truth-telling, as anyone in hot pursuit of a lover – or the object of hot pursuit – will tell you.

The Good, the Bad, and You

Who will be more successful – the businessman who insists on ensuring that everyone in a deal makes a profit along with him, or the one who does not hesitate to exploit others in order to flourish? Is cooperation a human trait found in our genes? Is exploitation a winning business strategy for someone wishing to maximize his gains? Or perhaps the contrary?

The answers to these interesting questions lie at the heart of one of the most volatile scientific debates of recent years. On the one side are our friends the economists, who argue that the driving force behind our economic activity is cold logic and the desire to maximize profits. On the other side are the evolutionary psychologist researchers, who believe that the decisions humans make are based on genetic models and patterns hardwired into our brains in the long process of natural selection. These models do not necessarily comply with economic logic but rather with the first order of evolution – survival.

Game theory, a field of mathematics, has been trying for the past fifty years to come up with mathematical models formulated like games in order to approximate various decision-making situations. In spite of the huge gap between the laboratory and daily reality, game theory has become the principle tool used by researchers from both scientific disciplines for hurling refined dirt at one another.

A study done several years ago might just determine the outcome. Robert Kurzban of the University of Pennsylvania and Daniel Houser of George Mason University in Fairfax, Virginia ran an experiment using the well-known game Public Goods. In a simple demonstration of the game, a group of fishermen lives at the edge of the water in a place where the fishing is limited. A quota on the number of fish that can be fished becomes necessary so that the fish population will not be completely depleted. A lone fisherman who decides to ignore the quota will improve his own situation; the others will suffer, but only marginally so. However, if a number of fishermen do the same, everyone will suffer, including those fishermen themselves. Similarly, if only a few individuals fail to pay income tax then they will do well at public expense, but if the majority of the public abstains from paying then everyone is punished by the decline of public services. This is really just the prisoner's dilemma in its plural form.

In an experiment they designed, Kurzban and Houser formed groups of four from eighty-four players who did not know one another to play a game via computer. Each player received fifty virtual tokens that could be traded in for money at the end of the game. In the first stage of the game, each participant was asked to decide how many tokens he would keep for himself and how many he would transfer to the kitty. After that, the game continued randomly for several rounds. At the end of every round each participant was asked to decide if he would like to add to or take back from his deposit to the kitty, but only after being informed of the others' behavior from the previous round. Toward the end of the game, the organizers doubled the amount in the kitty and distributed it equally to the four players. This sum was added to the value of the tokens each player had set aside for himself. In the next stage of the game, each participant was teamed up with a different foursome in order to play again.

If each participant were to put complete faith in the others and choose to place all his tokens in the kitty, all players would double their earnings through flawless cooperation. If only one player were to put all his money in the kitty while the others did not, that player would finish with only half his original sum while the others – by exploiting his will to cooperate – would earn more than their original.

In essence, the players could opt for one of three basic strategies:
-   Always *cooperate* with the other players to enhance the kitty
-   Always *exploit* the collaborators and put nothing in the kitty
-   *Reciprocate*: cooperate with those who show interest in cooperating and exploit the exploiters

By the end of the experiment it was possible to determine for eighty-one of the eighty-four participants quite clearly to which group each belonged – the cooperators (13%), the exploiters (20%) or the reciprocators (63%). Only three of the players changed strategies from game to game and thus defied categorization. Most importantly, the game strategy of eighty-one of the participants remained constant.

The fact that the behavior patterns of the different players did not change from game to game reinforces the belief that our capacity for reaction has been etched onto our brains in a long process of natural selection. The economists in this debate will be sorely disappointed to learn that the game participants did not use logic and did not change their behavior to adapt to the changing makeup of the participants and new circumstances.

Still, this is not enough to determine the outcome of the debate in favor of the evolutionists. For that, one more condition needs to be guaranteed: a strategy must be determined to be an Evolutionarily Stable Strategy (ESS). This term was coined by the geneticist and engineer John Maynard Smith in the 1980s with the understanding that a group could display genetic stability even without all its members adopting this strategy. An evolutionarily stable strategy is one that, if adopted by most members of its population, no competing strategy can overcome. In Smith's own example, he assumes that there are only two forms of combat in a given species: dovish and hawkish. Each member of the population ascribes to one type of combat or the other. The hawks fight unrestrainedly, withdrawing only when gravely injured. The doves merely make polite threats but do nothing. If two hawks fight, they will continue until one dies; if a hawk fights a dove, the dove will flee; if a dove fights a dove, no one will be injured. Members of a population do not know who the others are in their community until forced to fight them. Populations to which these norms of combat (and other assumptions) pertain will stabilize at a ratio of five doves to seven hawks. The following description should explain the evolutionary dynamic that brings about this relationship: suppose that only doves exist in our population; whenever a dove fights another, no one gets hurt. But then let's suppose that a mutation occurs and one hawk enters the population. It defeats every dove it meets, so that quite quickly hawkish genes spread through the population. But now, each time one hawk meets another, one will be mortally wounded. And that is how the balance will be restored, since doves flee when confronted with a hawk. A complex calculation proves that the population will stabilize at 7:5 in favor of the hawks. In our example from above, the exploiters are the hawks. This population will dwindle quickly if they do not come across cooperators.

A population of reciprocators requires both exploiters and cooperators against whom they can react, while cooperators who meet cooperators come out genetically enhanced and reproduce until they are faced with exploiters. What determines the stability of this strategy's mix is in fact the overall evolutionary gain made by this group (in terms of genetic survival) represented in our game by monetary gain.

The definitive test in our experiment is, therefore, the rate of success of each participant in the experiment. An equal share of the gains – even among those who employed different strategies – ensures evolutionary equilibrium and its suitability in defining the Evolutionarily Stable Strategy. Indeed, in an investigation conducted by the researchers, it turned out that at the conclusion of all the games, the income earned by the participants was very, very similar.

In other words, if we relate to the participants in this experiment as representative of the variety of our behaviors, it becomes clear that there is room in our world for everyone: the exploiters, the cooperators and the reciprocators. Furthermore, the existence of these behavioral models one next to the other is essential in stabilizing the population.

This conclusive finding determines that our approach as a species toward cooperation is evolutionarily stable. This is a result of our evolutionary development and not a rational economic reaction. Under such circumstances, all that is left to the economists to do is get back to work in designing the next experiment in support of their side of the argument...

And as far as we are concerned, the consoling message that we get from this study is that the cooperators and the exploiters – the good guys and the bad guys – all come out financially the same in the end.

∽

Causes and Excuses

"Waiter, there's a fly in my soup," complains the diner. "Yes," says the experienced waiter. "It's the heat that killed him." This is just one of dozens of possible responses to the age-old joke, one of the best of which is "Lower your voice, please, or everyone's going to want one." I was reminded of the joke on a recent flight that was seriously delayed. Speaking from the cockpit, the pilot announced that the delay was caused by the fact that the aircraft had been late arriving from somewhere else – useless information that does not reduce the airline's responsibility one iota in failing to make use of their fleet, but which is somehow supposed to appease irate travelers.

This sort of event, which we encounter on a daily basis, raises a question: what is the place of "cause and excuse" in our lives and to what extent is our social behavior effected by the way in which the suitable excuse skews our judgment?

A brilliant study published in 1978 by researcher Ellen Langer of Harvard University casts doubt on the flattering assumption that we form our behavioral strategies based on information presented to us and on proper reasoning.

In one of her studies, a man (collaborating with her) approached a line of people waiting to use a photocopying machine and asked to jump to the head of the line. He used three different explanations in making his request. In the first he told the people in the line that he had only five pages to photocopy and asked politely if he could cut the line. In the second, he added an explanation that contained useless information ("because I need to photocopy these pages") since everyone was in the same position. The third was identical to the first but to this he added relevant information: "…because I'm in a hurry."

The result was that 60% of those asked let him pass them by in the line without any explanation and 94% allowed it when the information was relevant and meaningful. But only 1% less – 93% – were willing to let the man go to the head of the line even when the information was useless.

The study is important because it teaches us that in an encounter between two strangers, at least in the line for the photocopying machine, it is enough to utter the word "because" for the vast majority of people waiting in the line to give in to the request. Furthermore, it would appear that the presence of *any* excuse at all, regardless of the information it contains, makes us willing to suspend our powers of reasoning.

But hang on a moment. Could it be that the headlines in financial newspapers that attribute changes in the stock market to various causes also fall into the category of "excuses" and merit our attention due only to our desperate existential need to attribute cause to every event in our lives? The answer to this question naturally depends on the actual ability of headlines to explain the changes in value of financial assets and is hidden in the wave of studies that grew out of the unexpected collapse of the stock market in October 1987. These studies set out to evaluate the link between news and the ability to explain the dramatic events of the day.

Economist Larry Summers, who later served as Secretary of the Treasury in the Clinton administration, took part in the most famous of these experiments. The researchers set out to determine to what extent macroeconomic news – interest rates, industrial output, inflation – explain monthly changes in the stock market over the period 1926 to 1986. The results were that this kind of news, which is clearly meaningful and relevant, cannot explain any more than one third of market fluctuations. News of a one percent rise in inflation, for example, translated to a monthly depreciation of only 0.13% on the S&P index.

In a second stage of the experiment, researchers examined the effect of some fifty non-economic news-making events (elections, the Kennedy assassination, the Cuban missile crisis, the Japanese attack on Pearl Harbor, etc.) on changes in stock market rates. The dropping of the atomic bomb on Hiroshima, for example, precipitated no more than a 0.5% monthly change (the stocks rose). Perplexingly, it turned out that the most dramatic fluctuations in the stock market often took place on days on which there was no significant news.

The study concluded that even when taken together, political and international news with macroeconomic news can only account for less than half of the changes in the stock market. And this was only with regards to the most prominent news.

Thus, the rest of the headlines – nearly all of them – are nothing more than excuses. We need them to quench our thirst for explanations no less than the media needs them in order to keep afloat. For once, the media is not to blame.

∽

Drowning in Numbers

In May 2004, Sotheby's of New York sold *Boy With a Pipe*, a 1905 painting from Picasso's Rose Period, for $104 million – the highest sum ever paid at that time for a work of art. Journalists called the painting, which had been purchased by John Whitney in 1950 for $30,000, "the best investment ever in art."

The question whether art is a good investment has preoccupied many a businessperson, some of whom have even used their business instincts to parlay this hobby into serious collections that become part of their own or their company's assets. But the question remains: does it pay to invest in art?

The sale of *Boy With a Pipe* shows an Internal Rate of Return (IRR) of 16.3%, quite impressive even if compared with the 12.1% annual return that the S&P 500 Index shows for that same period in the stock market, but not quite impressive enough to earn the title " the best investment ever." Incidentally, journalists specializing in art are not equipped to calculate the IRR; if they were, they would have bestowed the "best investment ever" award on another Picasso, *Le Vieillard*, executed in 1903. That drawing was bought at a Christie's auction in 1991 for $9,350 and sold two years later at Sotheby's for

$23,500. The IRR for that work of art was an annual rate of 64%.

NYU professors Jianping Mei and Michael Moses tracked thousands of art deals over several decades to create the Mei Moses Fine Art Index. When compared with the S&P over a forty year period it appears that the two indices produce similar yields, as shown in the chart below:

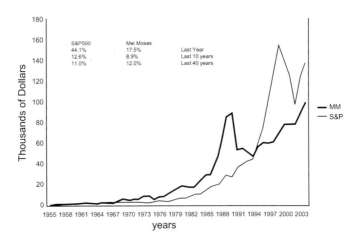

Source: Mei & Moses Art Index, 2004

If the stock market has blue chip stocks, then the art world has blue chip artists – Picasso, Monet, Renoir. Professor Moses analyzed 372 works of art made by these three great painters that have exchanged hands at auction since 1875. In terms of yield, Picasso leads the pack with an annual IRR of 8.9%, as opposed to 8.8% for Monet and 6.9% for Renoir. Picasso is also the only one of the three who managed to beat the Mei Moses Fine Art Index.

Still, this is not the most startling finding. That would be the fact that even Picasso, Monet and Renoir did not produce better yields than the S&P 500: Picasso lags behind by 3.6% annually, Monet by 4% and Renoir by 5.2%.

Moses and Mei conclude that the prices of well-known works of art are high to begin with and do not rise appreciably. They belong to the pantheon of international art, a fact already reflected in their prices.

That notwithstanding, there is still a way to enjoy significant yields investing in artists like Picasso, Monet and Renoir: by keeping paintings by these three off the market over a relatively long period of time (fifteen years and longer) they fare well on the Mei Moses Fine Art Index while still lagging behind the S&P 500.

Let's stop here to ask a serious question: what is it that causes you, the reader, to continue spending time reading these lines, which are really only a superficial snippet from an esoteric article I happened across in the August 2004 issue of *Art & Auction*? Is it my excellent writing skills? Hmmm, I don't think so. Were you recently considering picking up a Picasso? Guess again. I would like to suggest this as the real answer: you were powerfully attracted to what appears to be, at first glance, a detailed qualitative analysis of a financial matter, and if the numbers and figures that are scattered plentifully among the words are not enough to convince you, then a chart or two will do the trick so that you will be sure not to miss the promise made in the article.

And what is that promise? To try and put some order in your life – in this case, your business life. And why is this order so important? This is the crux of the matter: psychologists have determined that all of us (some more than others) are exposed at an early age to emotional losses and other wounds that have an effect on the way we function in adulthood as professionals and in life in general, the result of our parents' limited ability to give love, or social rejection from a peer group, or early failures (though they may be subjective) or any other reason. In a process too complex to detail here, the sensitive soul of a young person must deal with these stifling conditions while developing his or her independent personality in a way that enables satisfactory personal and professional functioning. However, the open wounds from our youth never completely heal, and the scars they leave behind continue to bother us.

These scars become the insecurity that characterizes all of us in one way or another. True, up to a point a sense of insecurity is an essential ingredient in the success of any entrepreneur or businessperson, but insecurity is also a disquieting feeling that we try to deal with by using all our spiritual and mental powers. Bringing order and gaining some control over the sea of data and information in which we are forced to float is certainly a first step in an attempt at illuminating our lives, thereby reducing the insecurity we feel when faced with such infinite dimensions.

Articles like the one quoted at the beginning of this chapter are geared precisely toward that deep need for order, for orientation, for a roadmap that will quiet our souls from thinking that the only sure thing is that nothing is for sure.

Our attraction to this kind of article is bigger than we are. Give us numbers, charts, graphs and tables and we'll be happy to stop reading other articles (not to mention good literature), the ones in which the potential for order seems limited. The naked truth is that nine of every ten articles that you read do not live up to expectations and do not enrich your life in any way. And still, you cannot resist the temptation and your eyes continue to float and hover over thousands of useless words in the vain hope of finding some secret – even a tiny hint will do – with regards to the rules guiding an unattainable world.

In his most recent book – *A Mathematician Plays the Stock Market* – John Allen Paulos reveals the secret, almost by chance, that "uncertainty is the only certainty there is, and knowing how to live with insecurity is the only security." Go on, read a good book.

Why the Mona Lisa Smiled

We live in an age in which half the world's population manufactures luxury products for the other half which no longer needs them for survival purposes. In order to sustain this global economic dynamic, ordinary marketing strategies alone aren't enough. In fact, the consumerism culture has already perfected the ability of business entities to take advantage of the evolutionary construct that has been hard wired into our brains for millions of years. We have been convinced that there are things we must acquire in order to fulfill some evolutionary deep-rooted need, when in truth we have been able to do without these things for many years now. One of the best examples of this process is *status anxiety*.

The use of status as a survival mechanism can be traced back hundreds of thousands of years, when we used to wander around the African savanna in small tribes searching for food and sexual partners. The leader of the tribe – the one with the highest status – procured the entire package: the ability to procreate, and the ability to obtain and distribute food. Those who were closest to the leader enjoyed secondary benefits, and were sometimes even able to supplant him (usually after a battle with other contenders). The status anxiety of today's consumer culture is just a more modern manifestation of the age-old desire to secure one's place within the group.

Let's be honest. When a friend of ours succeeds, we're mostly happy for him, but we're also a little bit jealous. This envy serves a fundamental evolutionary purpose: it encourages us to try harder. When we're jealous, we are more driven to attain a prestigious career, material comfort, a good marriage, all of which give us the economic means to sustain a family, which in turn helps to ensure our biological continuity.

Cornell University's Robert Frank, who studied this issue in 1980, found that most people would rather earn $50,000 a year and live in a neighborhood where the average income is $40,000 a year, than earn $100,000 a year and be surrounded by people earning $150,000 a year (assuming that the buying power of the dollar is the same in both neighborhoods). Since then, dozens of similar studies have confirmed his findings on status anxiety. These findings may be irrational, but time and again we have seen that when it comes to status anxiety, evolution prevails over reason.

This doesn't necessarily mean that we will be jealous of Donald Trump or Bill Gates. As can be seen in the research cited earlier, our immediate social circle includes only about 150 people – family members, colleagues, and friends from high school, the army, and university. The communal homogeneity that typifies these groups is responsible for the fact that whenever someone else has a little bit more, we immediately experience status anxiety.

Evolutionary history has a direct influence not only on jealousy itself, but also on the objects of this jealousy. Women tend to focus their envy on other women's beauty, since external attractiveness is an indication of youth and fertility. Indeed, as women grow older (and less fertile), they tend to become less jealous of physical attractiveness, and more concerned with status symbols that reflect material wealth, a sign that their mates are able to provide for them. Even a superficial reading of the gossip column confirms our hunch that the higher a man's status, the more potential partners he has.

Status is also a determinant of health. Recent studies have shown that when monkeys are moved to another group, and their status declines, they are more susceptible to arteriosclerosis. Oscar winners, as we know, live an average of four years longer than Oscar nominees who did not win. A study comparing senior government officials with their junior counterparts in England generated the same results.

Another person's success, then, elicits jealousy, or even hostility. In an evolutionary context, as we have seen, these two emotions serve a crucial purpose: they drive us to work harder, to be more productive. At the same time, jealousy has a distinct, and significant, disadvantage: it keeps us from establishing close interpersonal relationships, which are the very thing we need to maintain our equilibrium in our status-obsessed society.

This leads us to ask: is it possible to free oneself from status anxiety? Charles Nicholl's 2004 biography of Leonardo Da Vinci, who lived from 1492-1519, offers some hope.

Status anxiety was ubiquitous in the courts of Florence's ruling family, the Medicis. The lives of Michelangelo, Raphael, and other artistic luminaries were rife with power struggles. Michelangelo painted the Sistine

Chapel behind a screen to prevent his contemporaries from stealing his ideas. Michelangelo's envy of Raphael's physical attractiveness, social standing, and talent had repercussions throughout all of Italy, and Rome in particular. Raphael, for his part, used every means possible to persuade Pope Julius II to allow him to paint the second half of the Sistine Chapel, after Michelangelo had already started on the first half.

Leonardo Da Vinci was different. According to the well-known Renaissance scholar Giorgio Vasari (one of Nicholl's important sources), Da Vinci was something of an enigma to his colleagues. Sometimes he would work from sunrise to sunset without even stopping to eat, and other times he would go for days at a time without picking up a paintbrush. In a fascinating essay from 1910, "Leonardo Da Vinci: A Memory of his Childhood," Sigmund Freud analyzes the influence of Leonardo's fatherless childhood on his adult life. According to Freud, Leonardo's deep appreciation and understanding of art enabled him to detect flaws in works that others considered perfect. His personality was marked by a tendency towards lassitude and indifference. "In an age when most individuals were competing for recognition and personal achievement," writes Freud, "Leonardo's desire for serenity shocked everyone."

Da Vinci was universally known as a slow worker. The fate of his *Last Supper* was sealed when Leonardo realized that he could not paint fast enough to master the fresco technique, in which the artist painted on a damp wall. He worked on the Mona Lisa for four years and still didn't complete it.

Leonardo Da Vinci was the archetypal "Renaissance Man," a multi-faceted, eclectic person. At the same time, however, he can be viewed as a serial failure. He understood the principles of optics, but couldn't master the quantitative aspects of light. He designed the flying machine, but lacked the ability to create it. He left behind many unfinished paintings and untested scientific models.

Was Da Vinci afraid of success? Was he worried about his status? Leonardo, claims Nichol, was not upset by Michelangelo's gifts, or by his own inability to fulfill his scientific vision. Instead, he saw these challenges as learning opportunities. The idea that not living up to one's potential is a character flaw has only existed since the late eighteenth century, after the Age of Enlightenment. Leonardo may have missed out on major scientific discoveries – the force of gravity among them – but he did well in missing out on the age of self-realization. Leonardo succeeded where most of us fail: he set his own standards for success without ever comparing himself to other people (in his case, the brilliant artists of his time).

Is this gift unique to geniuses such as Leonardo? Can we, too, learn to judge ourselves on our own merits rather than by how we measure up to others? If so, the rewards are tremendous. The smile of the Mona Lisa – in fact, the smile of humanity itself – is reserved for those who have liberated themselves from status anxiety.

Information Is Not Knowledge

GOT and GAT are enzymes that penetrate the blood-stream only when the tissue to which they are connected – in this case, the liver – is damaged. A high level of this enzyme in the blood could indicate a problem with the functioning of the liver. Then again, a passing viral infection could have the same effect which would no longer show up in a second test.

A routine blood test I had done recently showed abnormally high levels of these enzymes in my blood, as did two additional tests done days later. After revising my will, I took my doctor's advice and did one more blood test two weeks later. The results were fine, absolutely normal. "Must have been a passing viral infection," my doctor pronounced dryly, handing me back my life on a silver platter.

After calming down, I could not help thinking that reducing the frequency of these "routine" tests would have saved me a lot of tension during the waiting period for the final test results. Was it possible that this extra information was not beneficial? Harmful, even?

Malcolm Gladwell, the author of the best-selling book *Blink*, has a definite opinion on this matter. He describes an experiment carried out by Brandon Reilly, director of the Cook County Hospital in Chicago, who was trying to solve the main bottlenecking problem in the emergency room, that of chest pains suspected to be heart attacks. The traditional method of assessment had a low rate of success, allotting quite a bit of time to taking the medical history of the patient and the various risk factors (cholesterol, weight, physical activity), as well as other details.

The revolutionary model devised by Reilly combined EKG results with only three variables: the level of constriction felt by the patient; the presence of fluid in the lungs; and systolic blood pressure lower than one hundred. The patient's medical history, diabetes, and even use of medications were not part of the equation. This model, which was tested over a period of two years, debunked the traditional wisdom in medicine in two principal indices that were being tested: this system detected 70% of those who were not actually suffering heart attacks and more than 80% of those who were and needed to be hospitalized immediately. All in all, this model was accurate in more than 95% of the cases. In retrospect, it became apparent that in a culture in which malpractice lawsuits are so prevalent, the doctors' need to protect themselves harms the quality of the medical decisions they make. Reilly got his inspiration from a study funded by the American navy in the 1970s that was designed to clarify which circumstances would justify floating a submarine (and thereby exposing its whereabouts) in the case of a submarine crewman with chest pains.

An excess of information can be particularly destructive when it relates to a period of high fluctuation. In such a case, the temptation to take action against the backdrop of anticipated change is great, even though the change may represent "noise" – that is, meaningless information that has nothing to do with the phenomenon being measured. In his excellent book *Fooled by Randomness*, mentioned earlier, Nassim Nicholas Taleb illustrates the cruel fate awaiting a successful investor who checks his investment portfolio too often, an investor who over-performs the S&P Bond Index by 15% annually with a standard deviation of 10%, enjoying a positive yield on returns in nineteen of every twenty years (that is, heartwarming odds of 95%). Not bad, right? Sure, until the investor is tempted to check his portfolio every single minute. The chance that a successful investor such as this one, with the very same portfolio, will be witness to gains at any given moment is only 50.17%; at any day, the rate rises to 54%, while the monthly rate would be 67%.

The bottom line on this phenomenon, called Noise, is dramatic. On the basis of one check per minute, we are confronted with thirty pieces of "noise" for every one piece of meaningful information. On a monthly basis the ratio is 2.32 pieces of noise for every piece of meaningful information, and only on a basis of once per year does the level of noise drop below that of meaningful information.

Statistically speaking, the more we sample the phenomenon at a greater frequency, the more we observe the variance and less the phenomenon itself. Emotionally speaking, we are not equipped to differentiate between noise and relevant information and are likely to err, taking action according to the noise and thus harming our performance. Daily exposure to a high level of randomness, with no emotional sun block, is the principal source of burnout and declining quality of life for players in the stock market.

In the late 1980s, the psychologist Paul Andreassen conducted a series of experiments among students at MIT that showed that an excess of news did not necessarily translate to an investment advantage. Andreassen divided the students into two groups, each of which selected a portfolio of stocks they were familiar enough with to be able to estimate their values. After that, Andreassen allowed one group to see only the actual change in the stock price, while the other group was exposed to a constant barrage of financial news and commentary that explained the fluctuations in the market and in the stock.

Both groups bought and sold stocks in their portfolios according to the information with which they were provided. The group exposed only to the stock price made surprisingly better decisions than the group exposed to news and commentary. Further, the more the stocks fluctuated, the greater the disparity between the two groups.

Andreassen hypothesized that the explanation for these unexpected findings stemmed from the attitude of the group exposed to a flow of information toward the bits of information with which they were provided. Each new piece of information overshadowed the previous information, which meant that the group members were giving undue importance to them – for better and for worse. News that accompanied the fall in value of a certain stock would create the feeling that the future would hold only gloomier prospects for that stock. On the contrary, the news that accompanied a rising stock created the feeling that the sky was the limit.

This over-stimulation led to excessive reactions with regards to the buying and selling of stocks by the students in this group. The overall scope of transactions made by the group exposed to a flow of information was greater than that of the other group. And excessive activity in the stock market, as dozens of studies have proven since the 1980s, is one of the most effective methods for destroying value.

So, what about you? How many newspapers have you read today?

෨

WHY DO SMART PEOPLE DO STUPID THINGS?

᭡

"It ain't so much the things we know that get us in trouble. It's the things we know that just ain't so."

-Artemis West, American writer
and humorist, 1834-1867

The Tyranny of Numbers

I am crazy about numbers, even insignificant data there is little chance of ever using to impress someone. I have this wild dream that I'm representing a client whose relative has been struck by lightning on a golf course. She is suing the man's insurance company, which claims that anyone holding a metal golf club on a stormy day has taken his life in his own hands. Well, let's see about that, I say in my dream: lightning hits 8.3 million times every day around the world. About 2000 of those each year wind up hitting a human being, of which 600 eventually die. At a flow of 10,000 amperes and temperatures that are seven times higher than those of the surface of the sun, death is instant. The chance of being hit by lightning is one in thirty million and that statistic has not changed in recent years with the increasing popularity of golf. My claims are irrefutable. The dream takes a turn for the bizarre, I will admit, when the insurance company representative claims that in a world in which we accidentally swallow eight spiders in our sleep during the course of our lives, everything else pales in comparison...

Years and years of business activity and reading newspapers have caused an extra organ to grow inside me, one that does not show up in x-rays – a tiny reality processor suitable for measuring, processing and presenting stock information, mortality rates, government allocation figures, sporting events, and just about everything else.

But the icing on the cake is of course percentages, the way they slice up and categorize a firm's profits, determine the size of the discounts on a shopping trip and even calculate our own life expectancies and that of those around us.

With time, this quantitative measuring of the world around us has become the main tool for defining it; that which is not measurable does not exist. Our experience is translated into thousands and thousands of numbers, tables, graphs and pie charts baked by a computer. And yet in spite of – or perhaps because of – the outstanding skill we have developed in quantitative presentations and analyses of numbers, we stand speechless in trying to answer the most important questions of our lives: where do we come from and where are we going? And, no less important: what will happen on the way?

There is no doubt that numbers provide us with confidence and a sense of control. When we are incapable of relating to the meaning of whatever matter we are faced with on a personal or national level, we are happy to fall back on the quantitative scaffolding that the media are so good at producing: the rate of support for a political candidate, the percent of rockets destroyed, the average number of cell phones per citizen. How, exactly, is this endless counting supposed to make us happier? Is it possible that with this relentless pulse-taking of the world around us we are allowing some important truths to slip through our fingers? Or perhaps we are actually preoccupied with counting and measuring precisely in order to avoid standing exposed before these truths?

"Now it's official," proclaims the television anchorman, as if some intuitive truth residing in our collective subconscious has been confirmed, or as if the latest assessment by some governmental department can replace a chapter in the works of Homer.

"The Tyranny of Numbers" is a phrase coined by computer engineers in the 1960s to describe the frustrating need to wire the growing number of components of a computer so that their power to think expands. *The Tyranny of Numbers* is also the name of a book penned by the British journalist and editor David Boyle and just what the doctor ordered for those number-crazed dreams of mine. The first story in the book is about Jedediah Baxton, an uneducated laborer during the Victorian Era who was discovered to possess remarkable number-processing abilities. After his first visit to a London theater, where he saw *Richard III*, he was asked how he liked the play. He answered that he had counted 5,202 steps during the dances and 12,445 words spoken by the actors. He had nothing whatsoever to say about the meaning of the play or the character of the charismatic and evil hump-backed king.

Baxton's counting was spot on, but the story is worrisome. Baxton is a good representative of the world in which numbers are everything but in which the deeper meaning of what is being counted and measured disappears. Test results have replaced intelligence, opinion polls have replaced leadership and average per capita wage hides the true dimensions of poverty. The constant roar of counting has created an emotional alienation that is the crux of whole civilizations that are losing their way.

Among all the other paradoxes that numbers engender, Boyle points to the fact that we can measure groups of people but not individuals. When we manage to meet Mr. Average in the flesh, we discover that he has strange taste in underwear and a humble collection of butterflies from the jungles of Borneo.

According to another surprising paradox, when we measure a certain phenomenon it tends to grow worse. The explanation for this is not clear; sometimes the definition of a phenomenon changes with time to expose a growing public matter, and sometimes people tend to report a certain phenomenon since it has become a matter of public attention.

The final story in Boyle's book tells of the bizarre U.S. presidential elections of 2000. In a country where statistical analysis is imbibed with mother's milk and the dissemination of numerical information by the media is the most advanced in the world, the fate of the president was determined by the improperly filled out ballots of fewer than one thousand voters. Suddenly it became clear how subjective and open to human error the process of counting and measuring can be.

Boyle sums up by claiming that this over-involvement with statistics and numbers brings with it a kind of blindness. When we measure life, we shrink it.

In the end, we have to admit that we don't get any thinner by weighing ourselves every day.

❧

Cutting Loose the Dependent Variable

Solomon Grundy,
Born on a Monday,
Christened on Tuesday,
Married on Wednesday,
Took ill on Thursday,
Grew worse on Friday,
Died on Saturday,
Buried on Sunday.
And that was the end of
Solomon Grundy.

This lullaby, from nineteenth-century England, kept hundreds of little children tossing and turning in their beds at night. Its dubious charm is a result of how our minds work; we assume that all these events were compressed into one tragic week, when in fact they took place over the course of many years.

Another example of a false assumption: in 2006, I visited the National Gallery in London to see the exhibit "Americans in Paris, 1860-1900." The exhibit highlights the influence of the Parisian art scene on the young American painters who flocked there in the late nineteenth century, including Cassatt, Whistler, Homer and Sargent.

Anyone over the age of sixty, as I am, cannot resist the ontological temptation to glance at the plaque on the wall and calculate the years between the artist's birth and the artist's death. The result, it seems, heralds the writing on our own walls.

A quick survey of the dates gives us the sense that the Parisian atmosphere is conducive to a long life. The life spans depicted on the ornate walls of the National Gallery seemed to be longer than the norm for that time. As soon as I noticed this discrepancy, I bought the catalog, did the math, and found that, indeed, the average life expectancy of the 34 artists featured in the gallery was 71 years, as compared to a life expectancy of 48 among the general population of Europe in 1900.

Could it be that the thrill of accomplishment, creativity, and public acknowledgement leads to a longer life?

Although I've always assumed that an artist lengthens his life with creativity and shortens it with alcohol, I know that this statistical association is not enough to resolve this issue. Consider the following example: it appears that the increase in wireless communication in England during the 1950s increased in proportion to the number of admissions to mental hospitals at the same time and place. What does this tell us? Nothing, really, once we understand that the natural increase in population growth is responsible for both of these phenomena. That is the extent of their connection.

Our desperate need to connect cause and effect gave rise to what is commonly known as the statistical correlation. In many cases, however, including the communications case described above, cause and effect are only indirectly related, and the standard statistical approach is incapable of detecting this.

For example, prose writers have a longer life span than poets. James Kaufman of the University of California compared the life spans of 1,987 writers and poets from the last few centuries. He discovered that, on average, writers died at the age of 66, playwrights at 63, and poets at only 62. How do we account for this difference? Some claim that poets are more prone to depression, and therefore consume more alcohol and other mood-altering drugs that shorten their lives. Others argue that writers often publish their masterpieces at a later age, while poets do their best work at a young age. Thus, anyone who dies young and has written a poem will be classified as a dead poet, while a prose writer who dies young will probably not be recognized as an artist at all. Most likely, there is some truth in both these explanations. However, the most convincing explanation is far less romantic: poets earn less than writers, and nutrition and medical care are both functions of income. This is the hidden connection between the two.

In another study, researchers compared the life spans of popes to the life spans of court painters who lived between 1200 and 1900. According to this study, the popes, on average, lived five years longer than the painters. In an attempt to take into consideration the fact that popes tend to be elected at an advanced age, researchers included only those painters who were still alive when their popes were inaugurated. The study, which included 80 popes and 426 painters, showed that the painters were 50% more likely to die before age 70 than the popes who lived at the same time. Even in this case, however, we cannot allow ourselves to draw any rash conclusions until we have considered all the variables. The autonomous lifestyle of a painter, for instance, is much more dangerous than the puritanical lifestyle of the clergy. Moreover, some of the paints that were used during that period contained toxic amounts of lead.

Some scientists are constantly striving to simplify things by means of the statistical correlation. A German automotive magazine analyzed the sex lives of more than two thousand of its readers. The dependent variable was how many times a week the readers had sexual relations. The independent variable was the kind of car they owned. Men who owned Porsches lagged at the bottom of the list, with a score of 1.4. Can we make a connection between these two variables? To do so would be hasty. The connecting variable in this case is age: most Porsche owners are older, and as a result less sexually active. As the writer and journalist Greg Easterbrook quipped, "Interrogate numbers and they'll tell you everything."

The statistical correlation is also the basis for most economic decisions, which try to draw a connection between two seemingly unrelated variables. The human mind does not want to consider that the two variables may, in fact, not be related at all. When a causal connection doesn't exist, we create it ourselves.

What really drives us to recklessly impose logical connections between two statistical phenomena? Undoubtedly, there is great comfort in the notion that the world around us is an orderly place, and that – despite all evidence to the contrary – we are able to control it. But the real explanation lies, once again, in the nascent field of evolutionary psychology. Our evolutionary roots reward our minds for quick reasoning, especially in a life-threatening situation. The ability to identify a predator's shadow, or to predict a famine based on the color of the soil, could save a person's life. In a similar vein, society fosters our innate desire to make connections between two variables, even when reason warns us to be skeptical. When we make an association, the rewards are many: a pat on the back from a friend, a nod from a colleague, or a winning argument in a successful but scientifically questionable advertising campaign.

The temptation to make a quick and apparently meaningful quantitative association isn't going away any time soon. But take heed: the word "figure" and the word "fictitious" both come from the same Latin root. So *fingere* – watch out!

The Odds Have It

The law of conservation of energy gives physicists the peace of mind that is available only to those who have accepted the fact that there is no such thing as something coming from nothing. Potential energy can switch to kinetic energy and kinetic energy can switch to thermal energy, but at any given moment the total sum of energy remains constant.

In contrast, "something from nothing" is the holy grail of the business world. Eager entrepreneurs build businesses from what was only a short time earlier a few pages of a business plan. Investment bankers are vociferous in their claims that the sum of the parts is greater than the whole, especially when they are trying to convince stubborn CEOs to merge their businesses.

Now here's a little magic trick to think about: A famous survey has determined that the average man is indifferent to the choice between a 1% chance of winning $200 and the possibility of receiving an assured sum of $10. He attaches more value to that lone percentage point of winning than its real value (1% x 200 = $2). At the same time, the average man is indifferent to the choice between a 99% chance of winning $200 and receiving an assured sum of $188. Here too, unexpectedly, he is willing to pass up $12 in order to secure his winnings. The expected cost of security is, again, only $2, or (1-0.99) x 200. In other words, people relate to probability in a way that the first percent (of 200) is worth $10 and the last, $12. But hang on a minute: according to this strange calculation, the other 98% equals $178 and not $196 (0.98 x 200), as any novice statistician could tell you. Where did those $18 go ($196 - $178)?

That is the work of alchemists in the business world, where something comes from nothing. The source of this strange human phenomenon is in our tendency to overestimate low chances and underestimate high ones. We credit low odds with greater value than is justified and the opposite with high odds. This phenomenon has a particularly positive effect on the balance sheets of companies in two huge sectors: insurance and gambling. That is where you'll find those missing dollars from the previous experiment.

Both the gambling and insurance industries are based on the overestimation of low odds, while the latter is also based on the opposite. On the one hand, the insured are too often prepared to buy peace of mind at a price that does not reflect the tiny chance of something happening. On the other hand, we tend to underestimate the odds – which are high to start with – that we will not even need the services of an insurance company.

Under these circumstances we are prepared to buy peace of mind at a price that no longer reflects the true probability of something specific taking place. "I want to sleep well at night" is an emotional asset, the price of which we are prepared to pay without regard for the quantitative laws of economics. Quite frankly, if you were given a 99% chance of winning $100,000, wouldn't you be willing to pay more than $1000 (the expectancy of the risk not to win) in order to sleep peacefully and avoid the possibility that you will miss a chance to win?

Incidentally, women are more likely to underestimate high odds than men, leading to a higher level of pessimism than men when it comes to the likelihood of seeing profits from an investment and causing them to be more cautious investors.

In 1995 alone, Americans dished out $8 billion for worthless life insurance policies, some 10% of all the policies bought that year. People purchased flight insurance and insurance for rare diseases and other kinds of insurance, all of which have nearly a zero chance of occurring. However, these are the events reported by the news media, causing the viewing public to believe in a real threat. Even though avian flu does not affect chicken that has been cooked, drastic reductions in the demand for chicken are reported whenever a broadcaster reports on some isolated case of the disease.

This irrationality is particularly prevalent in the behavior of the wealthy. These are people who can serve as their own insurance companies, or they can adopt the policy – usually justified – of moving to the side of the insurer through high deductibles. However, many do neither of these, preferring instead to overestimate the odds that they will, ultimately, make a claim. Thus it turns out that insurance, which was meant to serve those who cannot shoulder the burden of damages, is bought by those who need it least – the ones who can afford to pay the premiums.

The source of this phenomenon most likely comes from the structure of our human brains. While the right side of the brain is responsible for emotions and creativity, the left handles quantitative analyses. Apparently, low odds are not easily digested by the left brain and are probably swept through a network of neurons to the right brain, where they are processed emotionally and turned into a "story." "Today is my lucky day," or "God is watching out for me," are some examples of what people tell themselves as they enter a casino.

Anyone who invests in hi-tech has learned to immunize himself against the "story," which is part of any presentation of any new enterprise. The "story" has tremendous powers of persuasion, which can blind a potential investor to the naturally low chances of any start-up.

In a study conducted in 2001 called "Money, Kisses, and Electric Shocks," Christopher Hsee and Yuval Rottenstreich of the University of Chicago discovered that this model of exaggerating the assessment of low probabilities and underestimating low ones is particularly prevalent in emotionally charged situations.

A group of students was asked to choose between kissing their favorite movie star and receiving $50 in cash. Most preferred the money. But when another group was asked to choose between a lottery offering a 1% chance of meeting and kissing that favorite movie star and participating in a lottery offering a 1% chance of winning $50 in cash, most opted to take a chance on the movie star.

The researchers claim that in emotionally charged situations (and this lottery fits the description), we tend to react according to the feeling that each of us conjures up from the possible scenarios. In this case, the choice is between an exciting kiss with a movie star and an uninspiring lump of cash.

And what about our daily business life? How can we prevent ourselves from making mistakes connected to probabilities and emotionally charged situations? The solution is relatively simple: it is necessary to separate between two steps in the decision-making process. One manager should determine the odds of succeeding or failing in a certain line of action while another makes the actual decision on the basis of the assessments made. Luck, as is known, favors the one who is best prepared.

Anchors Aweigh!

Let's see if you can guess which variable has more of an effect on negotiations than any other. Is it well-developed business intelligence? Rarely. The exceptional patience displayed by one of the sides in the negotiation? That always helps, but not decisively so. Perhaps familiarity of the two sides? That happens, too, but not with any regularity.

So then, which variable is it? The answer: the initial offer. Whether you are buying or selling, whether the price is the only element in the deal or one of several, the initial offer as made by one of the sides is the determining factor for the results of the negotiations.

The reason for this, in terms of behavioral sciences, is that the initial offer is the "anchor." By making it, the one offering it is anchoring his partner in negotiations. Anchoring is one of the strongest phenomena in our financial thinking and affects the way we buy, save, borrow and invest. The power of anchoring is especially strong since we are more often than not unaware of its existence.

In order to understand this phenomenon thoroughly, read the following and try to answer the two questions below: Omar Khayyam is the most famous among the fabled Arab mathematicians. The discovery of zero, which enabled a great breakthrough in algebra, is attributed to him (as is The Rubaiyat, a collection of astonishingly beautiful poetry).

1. Did the events described above take place 282 years before or 282 years after the Common Era?

2. In what year did Omar Khayyam die?

The first question, as you undoubtedly guessed, is nothing but a diversionary tactic. Its only purpose was to plant a number in your head. In fact, 2-8-2 are the last three digits of the telephone in my office. You probably figured that 282 CE was a little early for the invention of the zero since there is no Roman numeral to represent zero, and Rome was destroyed after 282. Still, when you try to come up with a more exact number, like the one you are asked to provide in the second question, you will discover that 282 has taken up residence in your brain and pulled down the quantitative value of your answer. The result is that your guess will be too low, too close to 282, when in fact Omar Khayyam probably died in the year 1131.

So what exactly is going on here? The number 282, which was featured in the first question, has no relevance in the answer to the second question. But when we try to estimate a numerical value that we are completely uncertain about, our brains tend to relate to the most recent number to which we have been exposed as if it is relevant, even though in reality it has no bearing whatsoever on this matter. Ladies and gentlemen, I give you the anchor!

Daniel Kahneman and Amos Tversky, who were largely responsible for laying the foundations for research on our behavioral biases with regards to the financial decisions we make, conducted the following experiment:

They presented a group of students with a wheel of fortune on which were written the numbers 1 to 100. After spinning the wheel and announcing the number on which the wheel landed, the researchers asked "What is the percentage of African countries represented in the United Nations?" Naturally, there is absolutely no connection between the two numbers, but to their surprise, in the group in which the wheel stopped on the number 10, the answer averaged at 25%; in the group in which the wheel of fortune number was 65, the average answer was 45%. Similar results were obtained in subsequent experiments. The number on which the wheel of fortune landed became the anchor for the respondents' answers to the question of African representation in the United Nations.

Our financial lives are full of anchors, especially in areas removed from our fields of expertise. For example, when you consider buying life insurance you are particularly exposed to every offer that relates to the accepted levels of coverage and premiums. It is enough for the insurance agent to tell you that most people of your age have insurance coverage of one million dollars, which costs them $2,500 annually, for this to become the opening to your discussion. If you lower the comprehensive coverage to half a million dollars and reduce the premium to $1,000, you will feel as if you have succeeded in the negotiations process when in fact, both numbers might be high for someone of your age and physical condition. The insurance agent in this fictional story has dropped an anchor in your mind.

The annals of the stock market are filled with anchors. The price you paid for a certain stock is a very heavy anchor when it comes to the decision to sell it off. And what is the connection between the price you paid for the stock of a certain company two years ago and the value of the company today? Here, other factors that cause people to jettison rational decision-making are involved, such as risk adversity or fear of the pain of regret when a stock you sold rises.

Thus, whether we are aware of it or not, the initial bid in a negotiation process becomes the main anchor. Many businesspeople tend to believe that it is worth their while to take a bid instead of offering one since the received bid may suit them better than the one they themselves would have made. That does not contradict the anchor phenomenon if we keep in mind that the results of the negotiations will ultimately have been influenced by the initial bid, which could be better or worse than the bid not made, but in any case establishes an anchor and therefore affects the final results.

To wind this up, how can you avoid being stuck with an anchor that is too high or too low? The only path open to you is to maintain a poker face, ignore what has been said and continue the discussion as if you have heard nothing. On the other hand, if you relate to the bid you'll start to hear the rattling of the chains as the anchor you have become attached to begins its slow descent.

Siren Song

Anyone who has read one of Damon Runyan's books (*Guys and Dolls*, for example) knows that horserace gamblers always bet on a story more than they bet on a flesh and blood horse. In other words, according to Runyan, there are horses that don't win races even when they are the only horse competing, just as there are fired-up horses that win even if they drag their bellies on the ground the entire race. The names of both types of horses are whispered in stories told before every bet placed.

In a rational world, we should first gather all the facts, analyze them and come to a decision. In the real world, as many of us know, we already fail at the information gathering stage because of our tendency to prefer the data that support our initial position.

The real world presents an additional difference, one that is much more meaningful for someone considering making an investment. While in the rational world we are supposed to give weight to the importance of the data we have collected and then make our decision, in the real world we tend to skip over that stage entirely and go straight for the story, which we choose mainly for its ability to explain the data we have gathered and the connection between them. From the moment we adopt the story, it becomes the basis for our decision making and we give up on the rational stage of weighing the dry facts and what they mean.

Nancy Pennington from Chicago University and Reid Hastie from Northwestern have been researching the Story Model for more than twenty years. Their main hypothesis is that a person who makes decisions weaves a concise story that explains the data and from this stage forward pushes aside the inconvenient data and chooses to use the story to ground his decision. The decision-making process that Pennington and Hastie made use of was that of jurors.

In the most fascinating study among all those conducted by the two, "jurors" were asked to read the transcripts of one hundred closing arguments of murder trials. Half were delivered by the prosecution and half by the defense. The materials presented to all participants in the experiment were identical, but for one group they were arranged according to the chronological order of the story as described by the lawyers while for the other group according to the order in which the witnesses gave their testimony.

The importance of the order turned out to be far-reaching. When the prosecution presented the evidence in a story-like manner and the defense presented the evidence according to the order of the witnesses, 78% of the jurors returned a guilty verdict. When the roles were reversed and the defense presented the story while the prosecution worked according to the order of the testimonies, only 31% of the jurors voted guilty.

Investors, it turns out, are not so different from jurors. A study conducted in 1997 examined the effect of rumors on financial markets. For the purposes of the study, the researchers set up two stock markets. The investors of the first were fed news flashes while the investors of the other were supplied with rumors. In spite of the fact that the participants in the experiment claimed they were unaffected by the rumors, their activities proved otherwise. When a rumor could explain changes in the price of a stock, that was enough for the investors to treat it like real news and trade it according to what they heard. These findings quite naturally complement the early experiments conducted by Pennington and Hastie. Like jurors, investors tend to prefer stories to facts. This tendency turns stories into something quite dangerous.

In the annals of financial stories that have always worked magic on investors, a special place is reserved for stories of growth – the growth of companies, branches, economies. The reason for this is very simple and basic: if today we could choose the companies with the highest rate of growth in profits over the next twelve months we could hit the market up to the tune of 7.5% a year, which is the actual figure starting in 1975.

On the other hand, if you blindly followed that magic growth formula and invested your money since 1975 in 20% of the worldwide companies (according to the MSCI index) with the highest price-earning ratios – a clear indication of anticipated growth – you would be lagging behind the index by 6% annually!

As for stories about China and other developing markets, there is a similar effect. In effect, if you analyze the connection between the growth of GNP of a certain country and the stock market yields for that country in the years 1988 to 2004, you will discover to your great surprise that there is an inverse relationship: the markets with relatively low growth rates produced the highest yields. The apparent cause is the fact that investors in growth markets pay a premium for stocks whose anticipated growth is already figured into the price.

According to Greek mythology, Odysseus orders the ears of his sailors sealed shut and has the men lash him to the masts of the ship to prevent him from falling prey to the song of the sirens, which threatens to destroy him. And what about you? What's your story?

From Portion to Share

"Would you like to hear about our specials today?" asked the waiter. "For starters, I'd suggest General Motors stuffed with goat cheese and wrapped in filo dough, it's really delicious; for your main course, how about our amazing Bank of America à l'orange, served with braised asparagus; and for dessert my personal favorite, a scoop of Adidas in a chocolate champagne sauce."

Does the waiter know something we don't? Absolutely, says James Montier, global equity strategist at Société Générale. Montier recently discovered *Mindless Eating*, a book by Brian Wansink, a psychologist at the University of Illinois. The book is a fascinating journey in understanding the ways our brain weighs the variety of decisions it makes in relation to our behavior in the presence of food.

Montier, who specializes in biases connected to investment decisions, was not surprised to discover that those exact same biases affect our eating habits. At the end of the day, it is the same brain that makes both types of decision.

Our evolutionary roots do not hold good news for fans of health food. We are programmed to appreciate fatty foods in preparation for periods of scarcity. The salt we love so well helps us retain liquids in our bodies and protects us from dehydration. And our quest for sweets stems from the need to be able to differentiate between sweet berries that are edible and sour ones that might be poisonous.

The dubious benefit of having too much information in the process of investing has already been discussed in these pages. Wansink and Montier add another element to the equation: the potential damage in excessive information. In an experiment known as MacSubway, diners at Subway and MacDonald's were asked to relate to their eating experience in quantitative terms. At that time Subway was making relatively large amounts of information available with regards to the nutritional components of the food sold in their shops. MacDonald's, on the other hand, was not offering any information at the time.

Of 250 diners at MacDonald's, only 57 had any recollection of having seen any information relating to the food they were eating. The numbers for Subway, in contrast, were 157 out of 250. But the truly surprising finding was the connection between the information and the quantitative assessment of the culinary experience. The MacDonald's diners believed they had had a calorie intake of 876, when they had actually eaten 1093 calories, an error of 25%. Subway diners, who were decidedly better informed in terms of nutrition, believed they had a calorie intake of 495, when the actual was 677, an error of 36%. As we've said before, information is not knowledge.

In one of the experiments, Wansink placed jars with chocolate treats in different places around the offices of the participants. Some were placed on their desks, where they were visible and accessible; others were placed in a desk drawer (invisible but accessible); and some were placed on top of a filing cabinet that stood six feet away from where the participant sat. These treats were visible but not accessible.

Analysis of the study's findings revealed that the importance of accessibility was paramount. When the jars of treats were placed on the desk, the participants ate from them three times more often than when they had to get up and walk six feet to reach them.

So what's the lesson for the world of investors? Montier claims that for an industry addicted to excess information, computer screens hooked up to the financial news agencies represent the availability of the chocolate jars sitting right on our desktops. Since availability leads to action – buying or selling a stock, for example – all this excess of activity in the stock market leads to one thing: underperformance.

The profusion of options to choose from can be added to the damaging effects of too much available information. In another study, Wansink placed two bowls full of M&Ms in front of a group of people watching a video. One bowl contained M&Ms in seven different colors; the other had ten. (In fact, there is no difference in taste whatsoever between different colored M&Ms.) Remarkably, those with exposure to the ten-color M&Ms ate a whopping 77% more than those exposed to the seven-color M&Ms.

A study conducted at the University of Texas attempted to investigate the influence of social pressure on our eating habits. A strong link was found to exist between the number of friends or family members with whom we eat and the amount of food we consume. When we eat with only one person beside ourselves we eat 35% more than we do when alone. With seven other people, we eat fully

100% more than when we eat by ourselves. With eating as with the stock market, standing up to social pressure saves calories and losses.

One of the well-known characteristics of the stock market is the unexpected appearance of "stories," especially prior to the issuing of new stocks and with fast growing stocks. Wansink found several interesting effects of "stories" about food consumption. He offered the participants in a study six different kinds of food on different days. Some of the courses carried very simple labels on certain days ("beans with rice") while on other days the same foods were more elaborately labeled ("Cajun red beans with balsamic rice").

On the elaborate-label days, sales went up an average of 27%. That is the power of the story. But that's not all: not only did consumption rise, but those who ate from the elaborate-label foods also rated the cafeterias in which they ate as qualitatively better and offering better value.

Nevertheless, the most important conclusion in the book is that there is a lack of awareness about the biases that cause mindless eating – and mindless investing – that could prevent us from behaving rashly.

The height of the challenge facing us can be found in what the researchers call "the tyranny of the moment." That is the moment when we first notice the candy dispenser or we are offered to buy a certain stock.

The only way to overcome the tyranny of the moment is by adopting strict rules and habits of consumption. For example, making sure that half of your plate at every meal is filled with vegetables, or clearing away the dishes quickly after eating, when there is still food (available and visible) on them. The parallel in the stock market would be investing in a stock with a price-to-earning ratio lower than, say, sixteen, even as the engines of noise and the generators of electronic information are making their best efforts to bring us a wonderful story about it.

Hoarders, Inc.

Brothers Homer and Langley Collier lived on the upper end of Fifth Avenue in Manhattan without hardly ever being spied by their neighbors. Their story took a tragic turn when, in 1947, the two were discovered buried under no less than one hundred tons of urban waste that had amassed over several decades: newspapers, books, furniture, musical instruments and thousands of other things.

Fifty years later, Smith College professor Randy Frost defined the phenomenon suffered by the Collier brothers as compulsive hoarding. According to Frost, a significant portion of society suffers from compulsive hoarding to some degree, and one percent needs professional help before they become as hapless as the Colliers.

We all purchase things we do not exactly need at one time or another, but hoarders have trouble getting rid of them even when it becomes clear that their usefulness is nil. They prefer to collect to the point that they diminish their living space.

Research conducted by Frost and R.C. Gross in 1993 found that the central justification hoarders gave for hanging on to a worthless object was that it might be needed in the future. Next in importance came the following excuses: the object is intact ("it's too good to be thrown away"); it has sentimental value ("it has so much meaning for me"); and it has potential value in the future ("one day it's going to be worth something"). Hoarders have trouble sorting through possessions because to them, every object is special. Hoarders sometimes feel that giving up an object or an article of clothing is like giving up a piece of their identity.

Sue Kay, a British psychologist who set up a non-profit organization that wages war on collecting and clutter, categorizes the different types of hoarders: those who save for a rainy day; those who are miserly; those who are perfectionists and fear giving up an item will later be shown to have been an error that brings with it painful regret; those who draw security from objects; those who are rebelling against childhood deprivation; and even those who hoard in the guise of being collectors.

A quick self-examination as to your own level of compulsive behavior might include the following questions: Do you feel compelled to add the free pen you received at a conference to the pile of pens already cluttering your house? When you pass a rack of magazines are you convinced that one of them contains a secret that will change your life, and therefore you have to buy it? Do you hang on to your electricity bills from ten years ago, from apartments you no longer live in? How long will it take you to find the following five items: your passport, an extra key to your home, your last bank statement, your doctor's phone number and an envelope and stamp? More than five minutes? If so, you can understand how it is that British citizens on average spend a whole year of their lives looking for things.

In a public demonstration that fascinated thousands of people in 2001, British artist Michael Landy got rid of seven thousand of his possessions that were first catalogued: photos, artworks, family heirlooms, even socks. All these were shredded to dust by ten skilled workers stationed on either side of a conveyor belt that carted off the objects. The only things left to Landy at the end of this systematic destruction were his cat and his wide-eyed girlfriend. "When I was finished," he said, "I did feel an incredible sense of freedom, the possibility that I could do anything."

Manfred Kets de Vries, a professor at INSEAD, has a special perspective on the subject of leadership and the dynamic of individuals and organizations. He successfully combines knowledge in the areas of economics, management, psychology and psychiatry. In his book *The Neurotic Organization*, de Vries finds similarity between neurotic behavior in individuals and organizations. The book describes five main mental disturbances: paranoia, theatricality, depression, schizophrenia, and compulsive behavior. Hoarding falls clearly into the realm of compulsive behavior.

Does De Vries' theory hold true for business with regard to compulsive hoarding? The answer is a resounding yes. Departments created to serve needs that are no longer relevant; production lines for products that will never earn any money; holding on to real estate properties where renting would make more sense; a bloated manpower quota; and intellectual properties that will never be realized – these and others are the "possessions" that financial corporations hoard. But the possession that most successful business entities are incapable of giving up is the cash in their coffers.

From 2004 to 2006 the cash reserves of non-financial corporations in the U.S. increased by 150%. Like individuals, who justify their hoarding habits with various odd excuses, companies, too, claim that political instability, the Sarbanes Oxley Act (which requires all public companies traded on the stock exchange to maintain a system of internal controls and an extensive reporting duties), and global tax planning are the true reasons for amassing cash.

Or perhaps, as with De Vries' theory, all we're talking about is the neurotic behavior of an organization whose senior staff has been infiltrated by a bunch of compulsive hoarders.

༄

Goalie, Stay Put!

Any soccer fan can tell you the importance of a penalty kick, which is a direct, stationary kick taken from a distance of twelve yards with only the goalkeeper to block the shot. Penalty kicks are used when a player commits any of the ten "direct free kick fouls" within his own penalty box or to determine the outcome of a tournament game that has not produced a winner within the allotted time frame.

The relatively slow reaction time of humans against the speed of the ball (nearly 70 MPH) means that the goalkeeper cannot know which direction the kicker will kick and so must decide ahead of time in which direction he will jump to block the ball. His decision is not entirely random; it will be based on his knowledge of the kicker's playing patterns and on the movement of the player's hips before he kicks, giving him a better than average chance of getting it right.

The penalty kick has fascinated many academics since its characteristics lend themselves to analysis according to Game Theory, where two players choose their moves simultaneously and only two outcomes are possible: scoring a goal or missing. Under these circumstances the area between the goalposts becomes a fertile field for economic research.

In a sport in which the average number of goals per game is only 2.5 and the chance of blocking a penalty kick is less than 15%, a penalty kick can determine the outcome of a game. Thus, the heroic efforts made by goalies are among the more dramatic events in sport.

It is hard to believe but a study recently published in the Journal of Economic Psychology claimed that it was better for goalkeepers not to stretch their limbs but to stay put between the goalposts. Miki Bar Eli and Ofer Ezer of the Ben Gurion University of the Negev and Ilana Ritov of the Hebrew University of Jerusalem examined the results of 286 penalty kicks made in senior league games and championships around the world and interviewed 32 professional goalkeepers before reaching this surprising conclusion.

An analysis of the data shows that in 93.7% of the cases the goalkeepers jumped to one side or the other. In these cases they blocked an average of 13.5% of the kicks. However, when the goalies remained rooted between the goalposts without jumping to either side, they succeeded in blocking 33.3% of the kicks. Even if they managed to predict to which side the ball would be kicked and jumped accordingly, their success rate would only reach 27%. (Politicians might find it interesting to note that the success rate for moving to the left is higher than that of the right.) In other words, in spite of the fact that the chance of the ball being kicked to the center is only slight, if in fact it *is* kicked to the center then the goalie stands a much better chance of stopping it than if it is kicked to either side. The result forms the optimal strategy for goalkeepers: stay in the middle of the goalposts and don't jump.

The researchers believe that the energetic but useless response of goalkeepers is rooted in the ramifications of the Norm Theory developed by Kahneman and Miller in the 1980s. According to this theory, when a certain action is the norm we experience more intense negative feelings about not carrying out the action than if we do carry it out. For example, a person looking for a name on a list reading from the bottom up and finding that name near the top will experience greater regret than if she had started from the top and read nearly to the bottom in the usual manner before finding the name.

In soccer, it is the norm for a goalie to jump to one side or the other during a penalty kick. So goalkeepers are condemned to feeling greater disappointment about a goal scored when they do not move than a goal scored after they have jumped left or right. This leads to the Action Bias, which is the tendency to take action even under circumstances in which non-action would be the most suitable policy.

Dr. Ofer Azar believes that the results of this study are applicable in many other fields as well. In an environment of no growth, for example, heads of state are likely to initiate economic programs just because they feel they have to "do something." A manager who has recently joined a firm often initiates changes because that is what new managers are expected to do. "You gotta break a few eggs to make an omelet," they'll tell you. But who asked for breakfast anyway?

In fact, there are few spheres in which a tendency to action is more harmful than in investing. "After spending many years in Wall Street and after making and losing millions of dollars I want to tell you this: It never was my thinking that made the big money for me. It always was my sitting." So said legendary Wall Street speculator Jesse Lavermore, who came out on top of the stock market crash of 1929.

Berkeley researcher Terrance Odean has shown that investors tend to trade stocks at a rate that is not to their advantage. He even gave it a price tag: a hit of 3.5% on annual yields.

But recall that it was the seventeenth-century French philosopher Blaise Pascal who preceded everyone when he claimed that "All men's miseries derive from not being able to sit in a quiet room alone."

On Regret

In September 1990, the offices of Parade magazine were a madhouse. Phones rang off their hooks and by early morning there was a flood of mail, much of it from irate readers who, ignoring the postal service, brought their letters in themselves.

And what had caused this sensation? An answer to a reader's mathematical question by Marilyn vos Savant, author of the column "Ask Marilyn." Listed by the Guinness Book of World Records as the person with the world's highest IQ, vos Savant demonstrated her intelligence each issue by providing readers with answers to their often esoteric questions.

The September issue carried the following question:

"Suppose you're on a game show, and you're given the choice of three doors. Behind one door is a car, the others, goats. You pick a door, say #1, and the host, who knows what's behind the doors, opens another door, say #3, which has a goat. He says to you: 'Do you want to pick door #2?' Is it to your advantage to switch your choice of doors?" —Craig F. Whitaker, Columbia, Maryland.

Since the question resembled a situation known to most readers from Let's Make a Deal, the issue became known as the Monty Hall Problem, after the long-time host of that game show.

Think about this for a moment. Has the probability of finding that sleek car changed with the discovery of a goat behind door #3? A vast majority of the public believes it has not. In their opinion, the chances of finding the car behind door #2 are exactly the same as finding it behind door #1 even after a goat has been found behind door #3. Thus, there is no point in changing one's choice of doors.

But Marilyn vos Savant thought differently. According to her analysis, the selection should be switched to door #2 because it has a 2/3 chance of success, while door #1 has just 1/3. If this answer frustrates you, you are not alone. The letters of protest sent to the magazine included those of well-known professors of mathematics.

Mark Haddon poses this very question in Chapter 101 of his delightful book *The Curious Incident of the Dog in the Night*. His simple approach to the solution leaves no room for doubt. The book's protagonist, Christopher Boone, draws a chart of all the possible outcomes and can therefore dispense with complex calculations of probability:

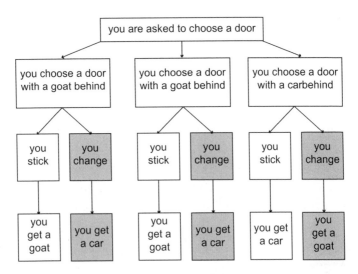

Source: Haddon, M., The Curious Incident of the Dog in the Night-Time (Today Show Book Club edition 2004)

Indeed, as this shows, if you switch your original choice you have a two in three chance of winning the car. Clearly, it is worthwhile switching. This is no longer a question of probability; it represents the entire range of possibilities and for two out of three possibilities the decision to switch pays off.

So, now that the mathematical battle has been decided, the question remains as to why people stick with their intuition, refusing to accept this reasoned answer even after reading it.

Most experts believe that this is due to a natural difficulty experienced by most people when it comes to probability.

According to these experts, we have trouble quantifying the value of the additional information we receive when the game show host opens door #3. Since the host knows what lies behind each door and because the last thing he wants is to spoil his viewers' enjoyment before necessary, he will always open the door behind which there is no car. That is the reason why there is a rise in the probability of finding the car behind the door that was not chosen and not opened by the game show host. When all options can be listed, as in the chart above, there is no longer a point to discussing probability.

I would like to add an additional explanation for the fixation of thought characterized by all those people who hang on to their original choice as if it were a life preserver. The source of this fixation may well be linked to a completely different human trait, the same one that keeps us from shifting lanes even though another one is clearly moving faster. The same one that prevents us from transferring money from our checking accounts to investments that offer greater potential returns. The same one that makes us indecisive about selling a stock, only to watch it plummet. Or fail to buy a stock, and sit by as its sky-rockets. What stands behind all these is our attempt at avoiding the pain of regret. For humans, regret is far more painful than loss. No one likes to lose, but the feeling that failure could have been anticipated makes the loss particularly difficult. Most of us will go to great lengths to avoid feelings of regret. Financial loss is a common price to pay for the fear of regret.

To demonstrate what I mean about the different shades of regret, try to imagine for a moment that for the past year you have been buying lottery tickets using the same number every time. A friend suggests that you change your number to your birth date. In the first scenario, you take her up on it, only to discover that your old number has just won. In the second scenario, you stick with your old number only to discover that the winning number is your birth date. Which scenario makes you feel worse? The first, of course. The pain of regret that comes from the result of having taken action (regret of commission), which nearly always hurts worse than regret borne of not taking action (regret of omission). In the case of the game show, the decision to take action by changing the status quo and switching doors creates a situation of greater responsibility for one's actions than the passive response of sticking with the original door. The more responsibility one takes, the greater potential for regret.

An unpublished study by Daniel Kahneman and Richard Thaler sheds light on the issue. Over one hundred affluent investors were asked to note a financial decision they had made which they particularly regretted and to define it as an active or passive decision. As expected, most of the investors reported that their biggest regrets were caused by the consequences of decisions they had actively made. All those who reported their biggest regrets from passive decisions shared a common denominator: most had a relatively large quantity of equities in their investment portfolios. This study shows that those people who regret opportunities they missed due to passivity tend to be those who take larger risks upon themselves.

Time also plays an interesting role in this issue. The claim that actively incurred regrets are more painful than their passive counterparts is only true in the short term. In the long term, it is actually the latter that cause more grief. Mark Twain expressed this best when he said, "Twenty years from now you will be more disappointed by the things that you didn't do than by the ones you did do."

In conclusion, the payoff is big if you can overcome the fear of the pain of regret. Unless, that is, you prefer goats to cars.

∽

Of Mice and Men

If we could include animals on the annual lists of the One Hundred Most Influential People, I would nominate a few pigeons and rats. Specifically, the ones that were used by B.F. Skinner, the father of neo-behavioral psychology, and the man called the "most influential of living American psychologists" by Time Magazine in 1971.

Skinner's most important contribution to modern economics is the discovery that it is possible to influence the behavior of rats and pigeons when we give them appropriate reinforcement after a particular action. Survivors of Psych 101 will remember that there are two schools of educational philosophy: classic conditioning (as in Pavlov's dogs) and operative conditioning, which is associated with Skinner's laboratory rats. In contrast to Pavlov, who proved that you can link an existing reaction (salivating) to a particular stimulus (ringing a bell), Skinner showed that you can create a specific reaction among rats and pigeons by rewarding them (usually with food) after they perform the desired action.

The temptingly simple idea that "If you do X, then you'll get Y" is supported by the principles of Western economics. Receiving rewards and avoiding punishment is, according to Skinner, the principal motivation for everything we do.

Skinner invites criticism from researchers and readers alike, because he is essentially invalidating the whole idea of free choice. From his perspective, there is no such thing as an "I" who is free to choose, and our existence is nothing more than our behaviors, behaviors that are ultimately determined by reinforcement.

Because of Skinner's findings, hundreds of millions of workers and supervisors receive bonuses. If in 1985 only 1% of CEOs in US public companies were compensated according to the price of a share in their companies, today it is the norm for more than 60% of these CEOs. Fully 85% of workplaces around the globe have adopted this reward system or something similar.

One of the more humiliating findings of the human genome project was that the genetic structure of humans is very similar to that of rats. Even so, how much can the behavior of a caged and starved rat, which only has to press the right lever in order to get food, tell us about the behavior of the entire human race?

In fact, the news is good. A mountain of studies from recent years has cast doubt on the traditional understanding of reward and punishment. For a long time, our economists, educators, and politicians viewed external reinforcement as the primary influence on behavior. Recent research in educational psychology, however, suggests that much of our behavior is determined by our internal ethos. According to this perspective, a number of factors influence our behavior, including a natural curiosity about ourselves and our surroundings; a search for challenge; and a desire to hone our skills and to reach higher and more complex levels of understanding. As is obvious, positive reinforcement – an external factor – is conspicuously absent from this list.

The use of incentives exacts an invisible toll. When a person receives a reward for succeeding at a task, he forfeits some of his autonomy, his sense of ownership. Because he is being judged by external, pragmatic criteria, rather than by his own internal standards, his self-image is damaged. Low self-esteem is a common symptom of people who are forced to compete for external rewards rather than internal gratification. An external award is based on obligation, whereas internal reward is based on pleasure. Hobbies are an excellent example of this phenomenon.

In 2000, Genizi and Rosticcini studied a group of high school students in Haifa, Israel; their results show us the limitations of compensation. The two researchers divided a group of 180 students into three sub-groups, and asked them to raise money for a well-known charity. Students in all three groups heard a talk about the importance of working together and raising money for the charity's activities, but students in the second and third groups were also promised a 1% and 10% commission, respectively. The members of the first group, who did not receive any bonus, raised an average of 500 shekels, in contrast to 154 shekels for the second group and 219 shekels for the third. Financial incentives, concluded the researchers, displaced the more effective influence of internal motivation.

Another recent study from Sweden examined how different rewards affected the willingness to give blood. Here, too, the incentive did not help, and for the women in the group, it actually cut down on their willingness by nearly 50%.

When a group of students was asked to solve some puzzles, the ones who did not receive financial compensation continued to work on the puzzles even after the researcher had left the room. On the other hand, those who were rewarded displayed no curiosity about, or interest in, the challenges. A 1992 study conducted by Teresa Ambile at Brandeis University found that professional artists are less creative when they are paid for their work in advance. Ten professional painters, who didn't know which works were commissioned, served as the judges.

Cui bono – who benefits – from incentives? Surely not the individual who is being rewarded. Mostly, it is the people who have never questioned Skinner's conclusions who believe in the effectiveness of positive reinforcement.

In some companies, incentives have replaced management. When people perform they are paid for it; everything else has to take care of itself. Management takes time, energy, patience and talent. Bonuses require nothing but money. Further, the claim that the routine use of excessive management incentives leads to improved performance has yet to be proven.

Let's test ourselves. Do we offer our children or our employees rewards in order to teach them skills, strengthen their social values, and boost their self-esteem? Or are we simply trying to manipulate their behavior? Ultimately, reward and punishment are two sides of the same coin. They both reflect an attempt to control other people. True choice is not between reward and punishment, but between a focus on external influences and a focus on internal influences. Even those who believe that the whole world is based on the relationships between the controllers and the controlled have to admit that a smile and a nod can have the same impact as a monetary compliment.

Patience may be Bitter but its Fruit is Sweet

The most famous painting by Hans Holbein the Younger (1497-1543) is a portrait of England's King Henry VIII. Less well known is his 1533 portrait of Cyriacus Kale, a German merchant. The portrait is typically Holbein, with Kale facing straight ahead, his arms barely containing the frame of his body, which seems about to spill off the canvas, and light coming from the right, which emphasizes the scar on his chin. The simple, straightforward portrayal of the subject, one of Holbein's trademarks, will characterize the many portraits of British aristocrats and members of the royal family who will pose for Holbein in the future. But wait. What is that in the background? Written next to Kale's head are the words "Patience in everything." Does Holbein know something that we don't?

Alexandra G. Rosati of the Max-Planck Institute for Evolutionary Anthropology and Marc Hauser of Harvard have an answer. In a recently published study they write about patience on the part of monkeys and humans, with the hypothesis that during periods when species adapt to changing conditions they must learn to give up instant gratification in favor of a larger payback in the future. While most species studied in the past have not shown patience beyond two seconds, bonobo monkeys and chimpanzees displayed a level of patience unknown to other species. Practically speaking, the chimps showed even more patience with regards to food than even their human counterparts. The humans involved in this experiment were offered tempting foods like raisins or chocolates. The chimps were offered the grapes that they love. Aside from the food, all the other conditions were identical; the choice was between receiving one portion immediately or three portions after a wait of two minutes. In spite of the fact that both groups preferred the larger portion, only the chimpanzees were willing to wait for it, often four times as long as the humans.

In evolutionary terms this is an important finding that points to patience with regards to food as a trait shared by humans and chimpanzees before the species separated some four million years ago.

In a different study on patience, people were tested for being able to defer the instant gratification of receiving $20 immediately as opposed to larger sums in the future. Participants were willing to wait patiently for up to 172 days for an additional $60, in contrast to their impulsivity over food.

This proves that while we may share some character traits about patience with monkeys, we have a greater capacity for patience in other matters – mainly decisions about abstract rewards as opposed to more concrete rewards, like food. Money fits this definition precisely.

The reward for patience in the stock market has been studied in depth and has led to the conclusion that long-term investing pays off. Nonetheless, the average amount of time that a stock is held in the New York Stock Exchange has fallen to less than nine months. One of the reasons for this is the accessibility of information, which makes us overconfident and causes us to act too often. Another reason is the incessant interest in money managers' short-term performance, who must give quarterly and even monthly reports to their investors. Under these circumstances, it is the clients who push their money managers – who do not wish to lose their clients – to trade excessively.

The appearance of new computer programs capable of high-level data processing makes possible the historical analysis of almost anything these days. A team of financial analysts at Dresdner Kleinwort Bank, then under the direction of senior strategist James Montier, conducted several such studies. They calculated, for example, that strategically, the most basic value strategy – purchasing 20% of the cheapest stocks (in P/E terms) from the MSCI index for Europe – would over-perform by 3% annually from 1991. However, if the investor were to continue holding on to that portfolio for five years, the accumulated over-performance would rise to 32%.

The explanation for this phenomenon comes from a pair of researchers, Kenneth Fama and Eugene Fench, in Migration, their unpublished working paper from 2006. In Migration they examined the U.S. stock market between the years 1926 and 2004. In addition to studying stock performances, they focused on the chances for "cheap" stock (in P/E terms) to "migrate" to the average P/E ratio of its corresponding sector and produce the desired "alpha" (a risk-adjusted measure of the so-called "excess return" on an investment) in the process. The chance of a lagging stock to adjust its PE to its sector average in the first year stands at 23% and rises steadily with the years. This is the main source of the portfolio's over-performance, but true patience is needed to make it happen. If only chimpanzees could talk.

౭∽౨

Danger: High Voltage

Go the mirror and take a good long look at your face. Pay special attention to the eyes. Then ask yourself the following question: Would you be prepared to send a dangerous electric shock to the body of some unsuspecting participant in a psychological experiment in which you are taking part, just because he was unable to repeat a pair of words that you read to him? I imagine that the answer is clear. So here is the next scenario: You are the CEO of a public company who enjoys wide-spread support from the board of directors, unanimous respect by peers and colleagues and the admiration of analysts. Would you consider passing off a certain large expense as an investment in order to improve the quarterly results for the firm, thereby putting yourself in a better position vis-à-vis the market and your investors? If by reading this you are hoping to get some positive reinforcement with regards to your character, you had better stop now because, based on the two situations presented, I have a certain assumption about your actual behavior, and the news isn't good.

While the second question is put to the test now and again in courtrooms around the world, it is hard to view the trials of Bernard Ebbers, founder of WorldCom, Kenneth Lay of Enron, Conrad Black of Hollinger and others as a representative scientific sample.

With regards to the first question, the chance that you – a pleasant, animal-loving, devoted family man who never misses an opportunity to donate to every worthy cause – would press the button marked "dangerous electrical shock" is more than 60%. I am sorry to report that I am no different.

The experiment was carried out by Stanley Milgram at Yale University. Receipts for electrodes, electrical switches, black rubber belts and audio equipment purchased in the summer of 1961, still on file in the university archives, attest to the simple accessories Milgram used to stage one of the most important experiments ever carried out.

Participants in the experiment were told it was being conducted to test the effectiveness of punishment in the learning process, when in fact the experiment set out to test the willingness to obey authority. Participants were seated in front of electrical switches marked with different voltages along with a short description of the level of pain inflicted by each voltage. So, for example, 45 volts was a stinging feeling on the skin, 180 a strong pain and 450, highly dangerous.

The participants were presented with a list of word pairs which they were to teach to pupils. A "teacher," dressed in a white lab coat, encouraged them to administer punishment shocks to "pupils" who got the wrong answers. Naturally, both the teachers and pupils were actors acting according to instructions given by Milgram. The pupils were told to increase the number of their mistakes gradually, which forced the participants to confront the dilemma that lies at the heart of this experiment: What is the maximum level of punishments a person will ultimately choose? With a rise in the number of mistakes the pupils were making, the participants raised the number of volts they thought they were administering. The pupils groaned, begged to stop the experiment and started to bang on the wall, all of this staged. When the participants appealed to the teachers for guidance, the latter would always calm them and recommend continuing with the experiment.

Remarkably, in Milgram's first set of experiments, 65 percent (26 of 40) of participants administered the experiment's final 450-volt potentially fatal shock. Dozens of similar studies that have been conducted around the world confirm the disturbing findings about obedience to authority.

In one of the many but lesser known variations conducted by Milgram, two psychologists were present in the room. At an early stage of the experiment, one of the psychologists disputed the other's authority and left the room in protest. All the participants in this version of the experiment refrained from using the highest voltage of electricity.

Milgram, who was considered controversial due to his methods, proved that the behavior of participants in his experiments was first and foremost due to the circumstances. With social psychology, your circumstances-where you are and in what environment is more important than who you are (your personality). If that is indeed the case, then when you take good people – the CEOs of public corporations, for example – and put them in dire circumstances, they will behave according to their surroundings.

But what are dire circumstances in corporate reality? Here is a partial list for starters: a board of directors comprised of friends and family of the CEO; shareholders who are limited in changing the articles of association and the memorandum of the corporation in order to influence corporate governance related issues; poison pills to block hostile takeovers and golden parachutes for senior managers – all these are central issues in crystallizing the corporate governance of a business entity.

Professor Lucian Bebchuk, a worldwide expert on corporate governance at Harvard, used such a list when he set out to test the correlation between the existence of a high level of corporate governance in a firm and its performance in the stock market.

Bebchuk found that a stock portfolio comprised of stocks representing companies with high marks for corporate governance on the one hand and selling short those stocks that ranked low on corporate governance attributes on the other hand, produced an average annual yield of 7.2% over the years 1990-2003. According to Bebchuk, purchasing the stocks of public companies that score high in corporate governance pays off very well for the investor.

Are you still standing in front of the mirror? If so, your last question is this: Why are you willing to buy shares of a company whose corporate governance is liable to turn good people into bad executives, and lose money along the way?

☙

Age Before Beauty

Malcolm Gladwell, author of the bestselling *The Tipping Point* and *Blink*, is the hottest property going on the worldwide lecture circuit. If you've gotten away with paying him only $50,000 for an hour's lecture, you must have caught his agent in an off moment. But in February 2006 Gladwell lectured students at Columbia University for free. His topic was "Age Before Beauty," the name of a piece he had penned for The New Yorker, where he had already been a superstar for several years. However, for the first and only time, the editor rejected a Gladwell piece. It was never published.

Gladwell spent the first part of his lecture on a rather esoteric comparison between two 1970s rock bands, Fleetwood Mac and the Eagles. After his detailed description of the two, the central difference in their success stories was easily discernible. While it took Fleetwood Mac more than fourteen albums and ten years to reach gold, the Eagles did it on their first album. Their fourth, *Hotel California*, is the biggest selling album of all time in the U.S. And where the Eagles were wealthy at a very early age (22), the members of Fleetwood Mac made their fortunes when they were already married for the third time, their kids were in high school and their hair was turning gray.

Gladwell's point became apparent when he applied the quantitative model developed by David Galenson of the University of Chicago to the two bands in order to explain the differences in artistic innovation between them. Galenson, a professor of economics and an art lover and amateur collector of art, was the first to research the connection between age and creative productivity. After analyzing the prices of thousands of deals made in the art world, he managed to present a model that could predict with relative accuracy the prices art would fetch when brought to market. He discovered that most artists produced their most expensive works either at the beginning of their careers (Picasso, Andy Warhol) or at the very end (Cezanne, Jackson Pollack). The former are characterized by being conceptually innovative for their time period. The latter became innovators slowly, over time, through trial and error, so that the bulk of their artistic contribution came late (Fleetwood Mac, according to Gladwell). Indeed, in an auction in New York in November 2006, a Cezanne still life painted when the artist was fifty-six years old fetched $37 million, while another of his still lifes executed when he was thirty-four brought in only $1.1 million.

So, why was it that the editor at The New Yorker rejected Gladwell's piece? For the very same reason that people in the art world do not support Galenson's model and for the very same reason that experts resent a black box mechanism even when it comes wrapped in proof of its own success. They would prefer us to believe that the process art experts use for judging is too complex, nearly magical, for us to quantify it in statistical models. Galenson's model is an example of the kind of model that persistenly takes blows at experts while those experts continue to prefer human judgment. Naturally, we're talking about their own judgments.

Another example has to do with neuroses and psychoses, two serious psychological disorders. Psychotics are cut off from the outside world but neurotics manage to maintain connection, albeit at a high emotional price. The treatment for these two conditions is completely different, which means that correct diagnosis is critical.

Lewis Goldberg of the University of Oregon has succeeded in developing a model that does just that. It is correct in 70% of the cases, whereas psychologists have a success rate of 60%. But the surprising part of this research is related to Goldberg's attempts at making the results of this model available to psychologists before they finalize their diagnoses. It is quickly apparent that although this model has improved the quality of psychological assessment, the results when taken together with the psychologists' assessments are still less successful than when taken alone. In other words, the combination of human judgment and this model is better than human judgment alone, but not as good as the model alone.

This finding is particularly important since one of the most common reactions to quantitative models is that they can be useful as a basis for improvement in the hands of skilled decision-makers. The results of Goldberg's research and that of others is unequivocal: the model represents the ceiling for quality decision making; any human attempt at improving it only brings down the results. One possible explanation for this is that the range of errors in a quantitative model is known and defined, unlike our own errors. Nevertheless, we tend to give more weight to our own opinions, even when quantitative models have proven themselves to be effective.

William Grove and Paul Meehl of the University of Minnesota looked at 136 different research studies that compare human judgment to statistical models. The fields of research themselves were quite broad and included achievement in sports, failure in business, parole for prisoners and even the reactions to shock treatment, among others. In the vast majority of the studies, the quantitative model achieved the same or better results than human judgment. In some of the cases in which human judgment proved more effective than the quantitative models, the people participating in the experiments had access to data that was not taken into account in the model.

Hebrew University researcher Ilan Yaniv adds our difficulty in accepting advice to this gloomy picture. Here, too, we tend to give extra weight to our own opinions and experience when faced with statistical facts. In effect, according to research conducted by Yaniv we believe in our own opinions to an extent of 71%, as opposed to only 29% for those of an advisor or consultant. A fifty-fifty weight would improve our decision-making abilities.

Why, ultimately, do we insist on making mistakes? What is the source of the over-confidence found at the base of most of the mistakes of human error recounted here? Could it be from our huge success at realizing most of our aspirations? Or from our talent in speedy quantitative calculations? Or perhaps it is our ability at creating perfect relations with our parents, our children, our partners? Yes, we've made a little money in the stock market. So what?

Money Managers: An Endangered Species

In 1986, Gary Brinson and two of his colleagues published "Determinants of Portfolio Performance." Brinson is mentioned in the same breath as Warren Buffett, and at the height of his career he managed $400 billion in institutional assets. The research carried out by Brinson and his colleagues is important because, among other things, the distance between its conclusions and your bank account is one of the shortest known in financial research history.

The three analyzed ninety-one portfolios of large U.S. pension funds, each of which had a history of at least forty quarters of activity in the stock market. The funds quite naturally adopted different investing strategies during the period investigated (1974-1983), a fact that was expressed in a relatively wide scattering of yields. The goal of the research, as is suggested by its name, was to try and ascribe the funds' activities to the characteristics of the investment strategies chosen and implemented. Among other things, the researchers looked at the effect of early planning with regards to asset allocation on the funds' performance. Asset allocation is a term used to refer to how an investor distributes his or her investments among various classes of investment instruments, especially what percentage of a portfolio should be invested in stocks, what in fixed income, and what in cash.

The results of the study stunned the investment community. The three found that no less than 93.6% of the quarterly returns were the result of asset allocation. Surprisingly enough, on a long term basis, only 2.5% of the performance of a stock portfolio was related to stock picking and only 1.5% to market timing. Everything, of course, was considered on the basis of long-term investment.

This groundbreaking research has proven itself since in many other studies, the most updated and comprehensive carried out in 2003 by the Vanguard group, one of the largest money managers in the world. The database of Vanguard researchers comprised no fewer than 420 mutual funds and their performance over a period of forty years.

Here, too, the funds' performances were checked according to various investment criteria. An important addition to the original study was to examine the various funds in comparison to a number of objective benchmark indeces and not only among themselves, as in the original study. So, for example, equity funds were compared with leading stock indeces for the same time period; and fixed income funds were compared with their corresponding indeces. Using the same disclipine, mixed funds were compared with weighted indeces reflecting a similar ratio of the asset allocation in those funds.

The results of the Vanguard study confirm the findings of Brinson and his colleagues. Like the original, this study explains that asset allocation accounts for 80% of the funds' performance, rendering the selection of certain stocks as well as timing only secondary in importance.

No less important is the discovery that index funds produce higher yields than managed funds even though they – how surprising! – are less risky. The rate of managed funds that beat the corresponding indices is not more than 7%, and at least half of this rate can be attributed to chance. Indeed, when the equity fund products charge a management fee of up to 2.5% or more, obliging the client to pay the transaction fees and always keep part of their money in cash, the chances of beating the market are slim.

In essence, the Vanguard study renders mutual fund managers to be an endangered species.

For its part, Vanguard took to heart the lessons of the study and immediately offered a wide range of index related products. Its index fund that follows the S&P is today the largest fund in the world. IShares, a subsidiary of Barclays Bank set up in 2000 and offering only index related products, has succeeded in a very short period to amass $120 billion (September 2005) under its management.

Is your money included in any of those sums? I hope so. From my own experience and that of brokers prevented from purchasing specific stocks for fear of using insider information, I know that this is a winning strategy. Nevertheless, I also know that you will have trouble adopting it. A surplus of confidence will undoubtedly stand in your way.

Overconfidence is that same human trait reflected in the notion that we know more than we actually do, and the tendency to dismiss the role of chance in our lives. Overconfidence is the trait that makes us certain we 1) are behaving cautiously, 2) are immune to something bad happening to us, and 3) are capable of knowing when to enter or exit the market and identify growth stocks before anyone else.

A person willing to squelch an ego bloated with self-importance at having chosen a winning stock by chance clearly understands that in actuality the ability to hone in on the winners is limited. Almost as limited as the ability to hone in on fund managers who can regularly beat the market.

So save yourself the trouble; hundreds of index funds around the world offer an answer to almost any mix of asset allocation. The question is whether you will be willing to succeed in investing while acknowledging that the only influence you will have over the investment process is the initial choice of asset allocation.

If you can, you'll find that with investing, like other areas, humility is worth its weight in gold.

The Average is Dead –
Long Live the Median!

The average is dead. University librarians across the country are eagerly awaiting the new statistics textbooks while the flag outside the National Bureau of Economic Research has been lowered to half mast and a grand funeral is being planned. The median, the shoe-in replacement for the average, waits restlessly in the wings.

The average fell victim to its inability to live up to the motto of its own election campaign: SIMPLE, CONCISE REPRESENTATION. In an interview that took place before it was elected, the average told voters that it "pledges to take responsibility for representing a group of lone values in a simple, concise manner that will enable speedy assessment of the approximate order of the members of the group."

The average's golden era lasted for hundreds of years. One of the best of those periods was the mid-nineteenth century, during the cross pollination experiments of Austrian monk Gregor Mendel. By laying the foundations for the study of genetics, Mendel enabled us to understand why children of tall parents are also tall (though not as tall as their parents) and why the children of small parents will be small, though, once again, not exactly like their parents. Scientists called this phenomenon "Regression to the Mean."

Physicists were the first to notice the average's flimsy grasp. They discovered that ever since the Big Bang, which created the universe 13.7 billion years ago, the universe has been expanding in a non-linear fashion. This phenomenon is observable as a larger than expected widening at the ends of the universe. The outcome of multiplying velocity and time failed completely in explaining it; Einstein's General Theory of Relativity came up with negative (dark) energy by way of explanation.

Economies, too, apparently expand non-linearly. The US GNP for the whole of 1835 is a sum now reached daily, as is the entire scope of international trade for 1952. The entire worldwide annual number of communication minutes for 1984 was attained several years ago in a single day.

This expansion translates directly into personal wealth. Economic inequality has been on the rise since the 1970s at a rate reminiscent of galaxies expanding away from the Big Bang. In 2007, for the first time, everyone on the Forbes 400 list has assets of at least $1 billion. The collective net worth of the nation's wealthiest climbed by $120 billion to $1.25 trillion. The top ten accounted for $202 billion while the top 20 were worth $335 billion. The bottom ten represented a mere $10 billion.

The main engine propelling this rapid expansion of the economy is compounded growth, which introduces an element of exponential acceleration not unlike the dark material that is responsible for the expansion of the universe.

To explain this, let's imagine twenty people in a room, one of whom earns $1 million per year while the other nineteen each earn $40,000 annually. Their average annual income will be $88,000 per person. In contrast, the median, defined as the number separating the higher half of a sample from the lower, is $40,000 in this case. Now let's triple the highest wage earner's salary to $3 million while the other salaries remain static. The new average will be $188,000 while the median does not change. In this sense, the median is more representative of the group in its entirety. This simple example drives home the failure of the average and the importance of the median as a "simple and concise" means for assessing a population rapidly expanding outward, to the extremes.

For that "rapid expansion to the extremes" – or, in other words, the economic and social gap – one need only look at those sectors that cater to the richest populations. In the past six years, manufacturers of luxury cars have increased sales by 50% (Porsche) to 75% (BMW), while other auto manufacturers have seen a mere 10% increase in sales. In this same period, 40% of the world's tallest buildings were built.

What, then, does all this mean?

Well, if you work in a government office charged with waging the war on poverty, I am sure you are well aware of the importance of the median in a population in which the economic gap is growing rapidly. If you are an investor, then it's about time to look into companies selling luxury goods and services such as auction houses, executive jets and luxury hotel chains.

According to physicists, the universe will ultimately stop spreading and be absorbed into a black hole. But it seems to me that for us it will happen much quicker thanks to the social gap. The post-mortem on the average may very well show its death was a suicide.

Apologies

Have you offended anyone lately? Forgotten some important date? Has your significant other been giving you the "look" or maybe the silent treatment? Or perhaps someone owes *you* an apology.

If you've been offended then you may be surprised to learn that you will not be able to tell the difference between a real apology and a forced one. Jane Reisman of Cornell University is responsible for the research behind this sad truth, which she published in a series of five articles in the March 2007 issue of the Journal of Personality and Social Psychology.

For one of her studies, Reisman asked sixty-five pairs of students to come to her lab. One of the members of each couple was joined by "Andrew," who was collaborating with Reisman, and the two were asked to work together on a puzzle. For each piece successfully put in its place the two were awarded 25¢. The other member of the pair was joined by another collaborator by the name of "Lynn," and they were assigned to watch Andrew and the other person complete the puzzle. A few minutes into the task, Andrew received a phone call and immersed himself in a gossipy chat instead of helping work on the puzzle. Even after finishing his conversation, Andrew continued to undermine the work of his partner in different ways.

When their time was up, Andrew apologized spontaneously in one-third of the cases. In another third he only apologized after being scolded by Lynn. And in a third of the cases he did not offer an apology at all.

When the experiment was completed, the true participants were asked to fill in a questionnaire indicating how they thought the money earned in completing the puzzle should be divided. The observers gave 34% to Andrew in cases where he apologized spontaneously; 31% when he did not apologize at all; and even less than that – 19% – when he apologized only after being scolded. Surprisingly, Andrew's puzzle partners (the ones most affected by his behavior) were more charitable: they gave him 36% when he did not apologize. Moreover, they were unable to differentiate between a true apology and a forced one. In two cases, Andrew was even awarded 40% of the total sum.

A follow-up study conducted by Reisman provides an interesting answer to this phenomenon. Participants were asked to read the description of an event in which an employee was late for work, leaving his colleagues in the lurch. In half of the cases the tardy employee apologized right away and in the other half he did so only after being forced. The participants were asked to think about whether they would accept or reject his apology and then rank their feelings about it. Participants who accepted the apology tended to rate themselves in a more positive manner than those who rejected the apology. Apparently, the main factor affecting those who were offended (and therefore suffered directly) and those who merely observed in the first experiment, was the same – both wanted to perceive themselves and be perceived by others in as positive a light as possible. The ones who suffered wished to be thought of as benevolent and forgiving while the observers wished to denounce the forced apologizers in order to show how they identify with the sufferers.

In England, where the word "sorry" is used 368 million times a day, one is told that this is a social expectation. In this context, an apology provides confirmation that social rules were indeed broken and this is the way in which the victim's status can be restored and social interaction can return to normal. The interesting question here is whether there is a difference between the behavior of individuals and companies regarding apologies.

Although logic tells us that any apology – whether partial or incomplete – should be better than no apology at all, research proves the contrary. Jennifer Robbennolt of the University of Illinois studied 145 responses made by professionals to situations that included some form of apology in reaching insurance settlements following accidents. Where there was a full apology and the assuming of responsibility, agreements were reached in 73% of the cases, and with partial apologies there was a 35% success rate. But the surprising statistic is that 52% of the claimants were willing to settle for no apology at all. The moral of the story is that in business, unlike with individuals, a lack of apology is closer to a spontaneous apology than a forced apology. So it is preferable not to apologize at all than to do so under duress.

The 2007 winner of the "perfect apologizer" award goes to David Neeleman, founder and chairman of Jet-Blue Airways. Neeleman wrote a personal letter to the thousands of travelers who were stranded for long hours in airports across the country due to snowstorms. A filmed apology made it to YouTube as well. He offered no excuses or defenses; he merely acknowledged the discomfort of his passengers and made a credible promise to fix what could be fixed by presenting a list of practical measures he had taken and by offering travel vouchers according to the Jet-Blue Airways Customer Bill of Rights that he wrote in the wake of this occurrence.

And finally, I'd like to apologize to anyone I may have offended in the past year. I am completely sincere, even though the people I've offended have no way of knowing that.

◦∾

Free Choice?

Every experienced restaurateur knows that the best way to get rid of a wine that nobody wants is to place it on the wine list one line above the cheapest bottle on offer. The reason, he'll tell you, is that most customers are not big wine aficionados, so when the host of the meal – the person who is going to foot the bill at the end of the meal – is asked to select the appropriate wines, he is unlikely to be willing to pay much for a component of the meal that he himself does not value; on the other hand, he does not want to be thought of as frugal – or worse, a real cheapskate – by his dinner companions or even the waiter. So he chooses the second cheapest bottle on the wine list.

American coffin makers have their own special slang, including the expression "third coffin strategy." Funeral home employees have learned from experience that when the family of the dearly departed comes to decide on a coffin, they tend to ignore the two least expensive models offered them, opting for the third. Not coincidentally, that third slot is occupied by a coffin that has proven particularly lucrative to the funeral home.

It turns out that these restaurants and funeral homes have been doing their clients a big favor by focusing their selections. Decades of research confirm the conclusion that most human beings are bad at the selection process, have trouble defining their wishes, and break into a sweat at the thought of having to make choices on a regular basis.

Most of us believe that we are free if given the freedom to choose according to our wishes. The truth, however, is that this absolute freedom of choice is precisely what destroys the gratification of a person presented with too many options.

In a study carried out by psychologists Sheena S. Iyengar and Mark R. Lepper at a high-end food market in Menlo Park, California, shoppers were given discount coupons for the purchase of jam from among six flavors. Another group of shoppers was given a choice of twenty-four flavors of the same quality. Unsurprisingly, more shoppers lingered longer at the stand with the greater number of flavors, but when it came to purchasing the jams, the picture was quite the opposite: 30% of the shoppers who visited the six-flavor stand bought jam while only 3% (!) of the twenty-four-flavor shoppers made purchases.

This finding would not have surprised Amos Tversky and Eldad Shafir. In expressing their theory of "Choice Under Conflict," the two researchers found that the tendency to defer or abstain from making a decision is directly related to the number of options available.

In a book published in the U.S. in 2004 – *The Paradox of Choice: Why More is Less* – sociologist Barry Schwartz attempts to explain how unlimited freedom of choice can lead to true mental anguish. Schwartz, a disciple of the theories of Herbert Simon, a 1978 Nobel Prize laureate in economics, knows that according to Simon, a business entity that tries to maximize its profits will most likely go bankrupt in the endless process of searching for the best option. Therefore, a business will "satisfice," that is, they will choose that which might not be the very best option but which will satisfy and suffice (in the business world, a successful decision maker is sometimes a person good at making decisions, not necessarily the optimal ones.) Schwartz fears that the enormous variety of products and manufacturers we are faced with as individuals has turned us into people trying to achieve the very best, something that Schwartz claims will lead us to suffering and misery.

How can we explain the fact that we feel more comfortable choosing from ten items on a menu than from thirty, or selecting a mutual fund from a list of twenty rather than three hundred?

Schwartz claims that the reason for this is the irrational way in which we assess the cost of the missed opportunity. Instead of comparing our final choice to the second best opportunity we passed up in the selection process, we compare it to an idealized mix of all the opportunities we were obliged to miss. A wide variety of options, barely inferior to the one selected, thus weighs heavily against the one option that will bring us relative happiness. As a result, we are likely to be tormented by the selection process or give up on it entirely, as Tversky and Shafir demonstrated.

Accepting the assumption that we have trouble choosing the option that makes us happy, we are left with two main possibilities for redeeming the situation. The first is to correct the entire selection process itself, and the second is to curtail the options we're faced with.

The first option is connected to Herbert Simon's distinction between those who aspire to the best and those who merely make do. The former include people who will not purchase a suit without first checking all suits and will not pay the price asked without first checking all prices. The latter, on the other hand, are prepared to make do with an excellent choice that is not perfect. The light that the aspirers eventually see in the process of their metamorphosis to becoming make-doers is the light of dawn that shines on people who are content with their choices.

As for the second possibility, we all make use of this option on a daily basis. We reduce the menu of thirty options to ten by what we do not eat – because we don't want something fattening, or hot, or cold, or we don't eat meat, or any other method for filtering. We tend to judge the people we meet by our first impressions, a cruel way of dulling the pangs of making difficult choices.

Still, as with businesses, the most common response by human beings to the unlimited culture of consumption is outsourcing. People read newspapers that publish comparative surveys, or they thumb through bestseller lists (the main purpose of which is to place limits on choices and discomfort). The wealthier will engage professionals, a consultant or a decorator who will fit the product to their personal needs for a suitable price. But most of us rely on the most common and least expensive method of outsourcing there is: branding.

The billions of dollars spent by manufacturers, service-providers and other organizations on advertising and propaganda provide us with an important service in reducing our freedom of choice to options familiar to us in the form of commercial names and symbols. When these companies promise high quality as well, the movement from being an aspirer to a make-doer is a winning strategy.

Thus, as a result of the ability to provide a solution to a real human hardship, brand names have become the most important force in the Western culture of consumption, and loyalty to the brand the most efficient tool for curtailing options.

I had a lot of troubling deciding how to end this chapter. There were so many interesting options, it made me miserable.

EPILOGUE:

Two Is One Too Many

On November 19th, 2005, a sparrow entered a hall in which a prestigious domino championship was taking place in Holland. The miserable creature knocked down 23,000 dominoes before being shot. A website set up in the wake of this event attracted tens of thousands of visitors.

In October 1987 the world held its breath while a rescue team worked diligently for two days to save Jessica McClure, a small child who had fallen into an abandoned well in Texas. Jessica, unlike the sparrow, was rescued, but the question that arises from these tales and many others like them is why stories about a single victim – identified by a name and a photograph – raise such compassion and interest in the media and touch us so deeply when millions of other nameless, faceless human beings are slaughtered, drowned or felled by diseases the world over but strike no chord in our hearts.

The above stories and the moral questions they pose are the core of Paul Slovic's unique article. Slovic, a psychology professor at the Oregon University and a humanist, titles his article "If I look at the mass I will never act - Psychic Numbering and Genocide". The title is taken from a statement of Nobel Prize Winner Mother Teresa who said, "If I look at the mass I will never act. If I look at the one, I will." Are her words a worrisome insight into human nature?

While there is no doubt most of us will pitch in to help a single person in distress, it is clear that there is no way to explain the apathy of political leaders without first understanding our own indifference to the suffering of others en masse. The cry of "Never again" that followed World War Two seems to have been replaced with "Again and again" (quoting an internet columnist M. Reynolds).

Many researchers relate to the "Dance of Effect and Reason" when they describe the decision-making process. Although rational analysis is important in assessing a situation, it turns out that our initial reaction comes from the part of our brains that is responsible for our emotional activities. Evolutionarily, it is the part that developed earliest, and its response time is fast and immediate. Our ability to intuit will always kick in before our power to judge.

Behavioral theories and a growing body of research support the notion that numerical representation of human life is incapable of describing the importance of this very life and that statistics about disasters on a global scale – as huge as they may be – cannot convey the true meaning of the horror and the distress or awaken our emotive mechanisms. And without this emotional reaction our logic has no chance of taking action.

One of the more effective ways of awakening dulled emotions is by adding a "picture" of some sort to the story. And of course the most representative picture of human life is the face. In a world of numbers and charts, it is the photograph of a human face that can make us identify with the downtrodden.

Although this phenomenon is well known in the laboratory, reactions to photographs of Rokia, a malnourished young woman from Mali, astonished even the researchers, Small & Loewenstein, who made use of them for an experiment. The researchers offered potential donors three options: to donate directly to Rokia, the victim pictured in the photograph; to give money to victims of malnourishment according to statistics detailing the scope of their misery; or, a combination of the two, i.e. contributing to the victim in the photograph where statistics are provided as well. Unsurprisingly, the photo of Rokia brought in twice as many contributions as the second option, but strangely enough, adding statistical information to the photograph of Rokia actually reduced willingness to contribute by 35%.

Tehila Kogut and Ilana Ritov of the Hebrew University of Jerusalem argue that the dynamics of processing information dealing with a lone victim of hardship is qualitatively different to the path we take in analyzing groups in similar circumstances. In an experiment they conducted, it became clear that willingness to contribute to a single, identifiable child suffering from cancer was greater than willingness to contribute to a group of eight (identifiable!) children suffering from the same disease.

So what number is too large, rendering the "others" as invisible to us? Paul Slovic and other researchers sought to discover the lowest effective number. They added Maussa, a malnourished boy from Mali, to the photograph of Rokia. It turns out that our capacity for developing feelings for more than one person is limited:

contributions for each child separately totaled more than the two together.

Bill Gates is known for his limited social skills; some say he is actually emotionally stunted. But though he may be a super-nerd, there are few people who can compare when it comes to abstract thinking about large numbers or understanding the problems of millions of Africans, which is where he has been channeling money from his charitable fund.

On that very topic, Clive Thompson wrote in Wired magazine in 2007 that "we tend to think that the way to address disease and death is to have more empathy. But maybe that's precisely wrong. Perhaps we should avoid leaders who 'feel your pain,' because their feelings will crap out at, you know, eight people…What we need are more Bill Gateses — people with Aspergian focus, with a direct sensual ability to understand what a million means. They've got to be able to envision every angel on the head of a pin. Because when it comes to stopping the mass tragedies of today's world, we're going to need every one of them."

But hang on a minute: Don't the leaders of the business world answer to that incisive definition?

∽

Do the Right Thing

In Mr. Smith's Shadow

"It is not from the benevolence of the butcher, the brewer, or the baker, that we expect our dinner, but from their regard to their own interest... We address ourselves, not to their humanity but to their self-love, and never talk to them of our own necessities but of their advantages... Every individual...generally, indeed, neither intends to promote the public interest, nor knows how much he is promoting it. By preferring the support of domestic to that of foreign industry he intends only his own security; and by directing that industry in such a manner as its produce may be of the greatest value, he intends only his own gain, and he is in this, as in many other cases, led by an invisible hand to promote an end which was no part of his intention."

These words, written by Adam Smith in *An Inquiry into the Nature and Causes of the Wealth of Nations* in 1776, laid the foundations of Western economy that we are familiar with to this very day. Smith, who was no stranger to considerations of social responsibility, used his manifesto to urge the cancellation of the privileges that the guilds and other professional associations enjoyed during the period before the Industrial Revolution. These were supposed to be replaced by market economics, even if that required government intervention.

Eighty years later, Charles Darwin presented his theory of evolution in *On the Origin of Species*. The theory, the scientific value of which is enormous, has a problematic by-product: anyone who followed Smith's line of reasoning that economic activities carried out in self-interest contribute to society as a whole was happy to discover that such behavior was also good for ensuring his own personal survival.

The combination of these two theories has had a huge influence over economic and social developments in the Western world. One of those – less obvious – is the ongoing erosion of the stronghold of religious faith, and with it, the most important factor in applying social responsibility: interpersonal trust. The level of trust that characterized most of the Western world in the middle of the previous century has (as has already been mentioned in these pages) been whittled away to nearly half today. The void left by the flight of trust and faith has been filled by materialism and consumerism, causing business to become the dominant power in the world. It is business that fills the government coffers and, in the age of global economics, the influence of business is so great that it can only be compared to that of the Catholic Church during the Middle Ages. The accelerated growth of the business sector makes it certain that this hegemony will remain constant for the foreseeable future. Achievements made only a few decades ago in the business world are now made in a week, and sometimes in a single day.

However, ecological considerations have clouded over the dream of Western consumerism in the past few years. If it can be said that humans have, for thousands of years, been shaping the earth, then today, for the first time, the earth is shaping humans. This is an excellent opportunity to examine the basic economic assumptions that Smith and others laid down more than two hundred years ago.

According to traditional economics, the price of goods are determined by the resources invested in them: the raw materials, labor, energy, etc. The level of efficiency at which these resources are put to use determines the manufacturer's skill in competing. In the simple world of the beginning of the Industrial Revolution there were no unquantifiable data in establishing the price of a product. The shadow price – the hidden and indirect costs of production – remained outside the equation.

A small experiment conducted last year in Sicily exemplifies the risk of employing across the board the belief in the wisdom of Smith's invisible hand. The red wines of the Milazzo winery have a distinctively earthy flavor and have won many prizes. In a brave and unusual move, the owner of Milazzo, Saverio lo Leggio, granted permission to a group of researchers from the University of Palermo to examine the 2004 vintage in order to calculate the effect it has on the environment. Lo Leggio was surprised to discover that a single bottle of the winery's flagship wine, Terra del Baronia, creates more than a pound of waste and releases into the air sixteen grams of toxic sulfides. The 2004 vintage alone – one hundred thousand bottles – produced ten tons of plastic waste and five tons of paper waste, not to mention the huge quantity of water wasted and the carbon dioxide emissions.

The upshot of the pioneering work carried out at the Milazzo wineries was that small businesses – "the baker, the butcher, the brewer" – are now recognized to be responsible for 60% of global pollution and more than

50% of environmental damage. It appears that the traditional economic model is not equipped to include the shadow costs of pollution. Scientific methods of assessment have long enabled the level of pollutants released into the environment during production of a certain product to be listed on the product's label, just as fat content, energy, salt and cholesterol are. Hasn't the time come for us as citizens in a consumer society to stand up for our right to be informed about the social and environmental shadow costs?

Cutting-edge companies have already learned that they cannot continue to compete only with regards to the price of a product or the service that they provide. They can no longer ignore the shadow cost of a product in terms of ecological, social or moral damage. The time has come for small businesses to tow the line, since while the consumer pays the price of a product, it is the entire society that pays the shadow cost.

We, society, granted businesses the legal framework to develop by limiting the personal financial liability of the owners of corporations, thus allowing the entrepreneur to take chances and enjoy successful results without risking his personal assets if he fails. But we have never asked anything in return. The time has come to collect on our generosity toward businesses and demand that they reduce their shadow costs before traditional economics disappears, and we along with it.

෴

Further Reading

Rich and Happy – Only in Fairytales

- Richard Layard, Penguin Allen Lane, "Happiness Lessons Form a New Science"

- Joan Duncan Oliver, DBP Publishers, "Happiness How to Find it and Keep it"

- Dennis Prager, Harper Collins, "Happiness is a Serious Problem"

- Paul Martin, Fourth Estate, "Making Happy People –The Nature of Happiness and its Origins in Childhood"

- Daniel Gilbert, Harper Press, "Stumbling on Happiness"

- David Niven, Capstone "The 100 Simple Secrets of Happy People"

- Fredrickson, B.L.(2002), In Snyder, E.R. & Lopez, S.J. New York: Oxford University Press "Handbook of Positive Psychology"

- Lyukominsky&Others 2002, 2001 "Responses to Hedonically Conflicting Social Comparisons: Comparing Happy & Unhappy People", European Journal Social Psychology 31

- Kasser & Ryan (2001) "Further Examining the American Dream: Differential Correlates of Intrinsic and Extrinsic Goals" Personality and Social Psychology Bulletin, 22

- Sheldon & Kasser (1998) "Pursuing Personal Goals: Skills Enable Progress but not all Progress is beneficial" Personality & Social Psychology Bulletin, 24

- Cohen & Cohen (1996) Life Values and Adolescent Mental Health Journal of Personality and Social Psychology, 71

- Diener, E. & Oishi, S (2000) "Money & Happiness: Income & Subjective Well-Being across Nations" Cambridge MA: MIT Press

- David Lykken "Happiness: What Studies on Twins Show Us about Nature, Nurture, and The Happiness Set Point", Golden Book Publication (1999)

- Brickman & Others (1978) "Lottery Winners and Accident Victims: Is Happiness Relative?" Journal of Personality & Social Psychology 36

- Myers (1993) "The Pursuit of Happiness: Who is Happy & Why", Avon Books

- John Holliwell, University of British Columbia, "Analysis of World Value Survey"

- Daniel Gilbert and Others (1998) "Immune Neglect: A Source of Durability Bias in Affective Forecasting" Journal of Personality and Social Psychology 75

- Deneve & Cooper (1998) "The Happy Personality: A Meta-Analysis of 137 personality Traits and Subjective Well-being" Psychological Bulletin, 124

- Myers (2000) "The Secret of Happiness" (Summer, 2004)

- Myers & Diener (1995) "Who is Happy?" Psychological Sciences 6

- Gibbons, FX (1986) "Social Comparison and Depression: Company's Effect on Misery" Journal of Personality and Social Psychology 51

- Gruder, C (1977) "Choice of Comparison Persons in Evaluating Oneself" in J.M. Suls & Miller (Eds) Social Comparison Processes: Theoretical and Empirical Perspectives, Washington DC: Hemisphere

- Suls, J. & Wheeler, L. (Eds.) (2000) Handbook of Social Comparison: Theory and Research, NY: Plenum

- National Opinion Research Center Surveys (U.S.)

- Historical Statistics of the United States and Economic Indications

- Psychology, 7th Edition, 2004, Worth Publishers, NY

- Mihaly Csikszentmihaly, Harper Perennial "Flow – The Psychology of Optimal Experience"

- Kahneman, Krueger, Schkade, Schwarz & Stone (2003) "Measuring the Quality of Life"

- Van Boven & Gilovich (2003) "To Do or to Have? That is the question", Journal of Personality and Social Psychology, 85

- Van Boven (2005) "Experientialism, Materialism, and the Pursuit of Happiness" Review of General Psychology, 9

The Black Swan

- Nassim Nicholas Taleb "Fooled in Randomness" Thomson Teyere

Fish Tales

- Bertrand Russel "In Praise of Idleness"

- Carl Honore"In Praise of Slowness", Harper

- SlowDown Now.Org.

Snowflakes and Success

- Angela L. Duckworth and Martin E.P. Seligman "Self Discipline Outdoes IQ in Predicting Academic Performance of Adolescents" Journal of Psychological Science Vol. 16 Issue 12 December 2005

Working Out with Polar Bears

- Mark Muraven & Roy F. Baumeister – "Self-Regulation and Depletion of Limited Resources: Does Self-Control Resemble a Muscle?" Psychological Bulletin 2000, Vol.126, No. 2

- Kathleen D. Vohs & Ronald J. Faber – "Spent Resources; Self-Regulatory Resource Availability Affects Impulse Buying", Journal of Consumer Research, Vol. 33, March 2007.

- David Adler, "Baby Steps to Grown-up Control", Psychology Today, Feb. 2007

Murder on the Investment Commmittee

- Darley, J. & Latane, B. "Bystander Intervention in Emergencies: Diffusion of Responsibility" Journal of Personality and Social Psychology 8

- Stasser, G. & Titus, W. "Pooling and Unshared Information in Group Decision Making" Journal of Personality and Social Psychology, 1985

- Stasser, G & Stewart D. "Discovery of Hidden Profiles by Decision-Making Groups" Journal of Personality and Social Psychology, 1992

The Riddle of Hungarian Applause

- Philip Ball "Critical Mass" Arrow Books

- Z. Neda, E. Ravasz, Y. Brechet, T. Vicsek, A,-L. Barabasi "The Sound of Many Hands Clapping" Nature (09, 200?)

The Admiralty Regrets...

- Warren, C. & Benson, J.Robert Frank, "Thetis The Admiralty Regrets" Cornell University 1980

Darwin, Inc.

- Grinnel, J. & McComb, K (2001) "Roaring and Social Communication in African Lions: The Limitations imposed by Listeners" Animal Behaviour 62

- Frans de Wall "Chimpanzee Politics Power and Sex Among Apes" John Hopkins University Press 1982

- Roger Fonts "Next of Kin: My Conversation with Chimpanzees" Harper Paperbacks

Firstborn Children are not Gamblers

- Frank J. Sulloway, "Born to Rebel", Abacus

- Dalton Conley "The Pecking Order: Which Siblings Succeed and Why", Pantheon

Does Trust Pay?

- Edward Banfield "The Moral Basis of Backward Society" New York Free Press 1958

The Truth About Lying

- David Livingstone Smith "Why We Lie", St. Martin's Press

- Dory Hollander "101 Lies Men Tell Women" (Harper Collins)

- Charles Ford American Psychiatric Publishing, New Ed edition "Lies! Lies! Lies!" The Psychology of Deceit

- Tyler, J.M. & Feldman R.S. (2004) "Truth, Lies and Self-Presentation: How Gender and Anticipated Future Interaction Relate to Deceptive Behaviour"

- Jeff Hancock, Cornell University "Deception and Design: The Impact of Communication Technology on Lying Behaviour"

The Good, the Bad and You

- Dawkins, Richard, "The Selfish Gene," Oxford University Press, 2006

- Daniel Houser & Robert Kurzban "An experimental Investigation of Cooperative Types in Human Groups: A complement to Evolutionary Theory and Simulations – Proceedings of the National Academy of Science 102(5)

Drowning in Numbers

- Art & Auction Magazine August 2004

- Mie & Moses Art Index

- John Allen Paulos Basic Books "A Mathematician Plays the Stock Market"

Why the Mona Lisa Smiled

- King, Ross, Michaelangelo and the Pope's Ceiling, Penguin Books, 2003

- Freud, Sigmund, Leonardo Da Vinci and a Memory of His Childhood. W.W. Norton, 1989

Information is not Knowledge

- Paul B. Andreassen MIT (1980)
- Malcolm Gladwell, "Blink – The Power of Thinking without Thinking"

Cutting Loose the Dependent Variable

- James Kaufman , California State University Journal of Death Studies, 1982
- The National Gallery London "Americans in Paris" 1860-1900, 22 February – 21 May 200
- Maria Patrizia Canieri & Diego Serraino "Longevity of Popes and Artists between the 13th and 19th Century"
- Mark Landler "Sex Cars and The German Psyche", IHT, June 8, 2004

Siren Song

- Nancy Pennington & Reid Hastie "Evidence Evaluation in Complex Decision Making" Journal of Personality and Social Psychology 1986, Vol. 51 No.2

- "Explaining the Evidence: Further tests of the Story Model for Juror Decision Making," March 30, 1987, Working paper #145-2

From Portion to Share

- Brian Wansink (2006) "Mindless Eating; Why We Eat More Than We Think" (Bantam Books)

- Painter, Wansink and Hieggelke (2002) "How Visibility and Convenience Influence Candy Consumption Appetite"

- Wansink, Painter, Ittersum (2001) "How do descriptive menu labels influence customers?", Cornell Hotel & Restaurant Administration Quarterly

- Bell & Pliner (2003) "Time to Eat; The Relationship between the Number of People Eating and Meal Duration in Three Lunch Settings. Appetite.

Hoarders, Inc.

- Sue Kay "No More Clutter" (Hodder Mobius)

- Manfred F.R. Kets de Vries & Danny Miller "The Neurotic Organization" (Jossey Bass 1984)

- Cohen & Cohen "The Paranoiac Corporation"

Goalie, Stay Put!

- Michael Bar-Eil, Ofer H. Azar, Ilana Ritvo, Yael Keidar Levin, Galit Schein, "Action bias among elite soccer goalkeepers. The case of penalty kicks." Journal of Economic Psychology.

Of Mice and Men

- Uri Gneezy and Aldo Rustichini "Pay Enough or Don't Pay at all" (2000), The Quarterly Journal of Economics

- Tore Ellingsen and Magnus Johannesson, May 12, 2006 "Trust as an Incentive"

- Carl Mellstroem and Magnus Joannesson "Crowding Out in Blood Donation: Was Titmus Right?"

- Alfie Kohn – "Punished by Rewards" (Houghton & Mifflin)

Patience May be Bitter but its Fruit is Sweet

- Alexandra G. Rosati, Jeffrey R. Stevens, Brian Hare, Marc D. Hansen, "The evolutionary origins of human patience: temporal preferences in chimpanzees, bonobos and human adults," Current Biology 15, 1663-1668

- Fama, Eugene and Kenneth French, February 2007 Working Paper

Danger: High Voltage

- Slater, Lauren, "Opening Skinner's Box: Great Psychological Experiments of the Twentieth Century." W.W. Norton, 2005.

- Stanley Milgram (1974) "Obedience to Authority

- Bebchuk, Cohen and Ferrell (2004) "What Matters in Corporate Governance"

Age Before Beauty

- Grove, Zaid, Lebow, Snitz, Nelson (2000) "Clinical Versus Mechanical Prediction: A Meta-Analysis", Psychological Assessment, 12

- Paul E. Meehl "The Limits of Scientific Raesoning"

- David Galenson "Old Masters and Young Geniuses

- Michael Lewis "Money Ball"

- Grove & Meehl (1996) – "Comparative efficiency of informal and formal prediction procedures" Psychology, Public Policy and Law,2

- Malcolm Gladwell "Age Before Beauty" A talk hosted by Columbia University and transcribed by John Lennox

- John Ruscio "Holistic Judgment in Clinical Practice"

- Goldberg (1968) "Simple Models or Simple Processes?" Some research on Clinical Judgment, American Psychologist

Money Managers: An Endangered Species

- Brinson, Hood and Beebowers "Determinants of Portfolio Performance" (1986) Analysts Journal Vol. 42, No.4 (July/August)

- The Vanguard Group, Inc. July 2003 "Sources of Portfolio Performance: The Enduring Importance of Asset Allocation"

Free Choice

- Barry Schwartz, "The Paradox of Choice – Why More is Less" Ecco

- Tversky, A & Shafir, E. (1992) "Choice Under Conflict – The Dynamics of Deferred Decisions", Psychological Science 3, 358-361

Apologies

- Risen, Jane L, and Thomas Gilovich, "Target and Observer Differences in the Acceptance of Questionable Apologies." Journal of Personality and Social Psychology 2007, Vol. 92 No.3 418-433

Two is one too many

- "If I look at the mass I will never act"; Psychic Numbing and Genocide Paul Slovic Judgement and Decision Making, Vol. 2 No.2, April 2007 pp79-95

- Kogut, T & Ritov, I (2006) The "Identified Victim" effect: An identified group, or just a single individual? Journal of Behavioral Decision Making, 18, 157-167

Causes & Excuses

- Ellen Langer, Arthur Black and Benzion Chanowitz, The Mindlessness of Ostensibly Thoughtful Action: The role of "Placebic" information in interpersonal interaction. Journal of Personality and Social Psychology 1978, Vol. 36, No.6, 635-642

ॐ

40942906R00159

Made in the USA
Middletown, DE
02 April 2019